"I'm pregnant." There was a moment where he could only look at her in bewilderment, and she continued, "With your baby."

Max rocked backward and tried to steady himself, failed and reached out to grasp the edge of his desk. He couldn't be a father. Couldn't...wouldn't. Shouldn't. His gaze dropped to her midriff, and for a moment, a sense of awe touched him, tried to thread through the panic. A baby, his baby, was growing inside Stella.

"I get it's a shock," she said. "And as I said, I'm not here because I expect anything. I know that you have marriage plans, but I thought you should know. Because obviously one day the baby will ask me who his or her dad is and..."

Her words cut through the electric chaos that was blindsiding his brain. He had spent his whole life wondering about the identity of a parent who had abandoned him, spent years piecing together information about a father whom he wished wasn't his father. There was no way he would, could or should put any child through even a fraction of that.

Dear Reader,

I loved writing this book. Stella stuck in my head from my previous book, *Falling for His Stand-In Fiancée*. She is Adriana's older sister, and the minute Adriana and Rob left my head, Stella was there asking for her story to be written.

So I did.

Stella is scared that her real self makes bad decisions that lead to tragic consequences and so she has built herself a poised, perfect persona to hide behind.

But one night with Max and her whole carefully planned life is changed. Worse, Max gets under her skin and behind her persona.

As for Max, he has never got over a childhood where abandonment was a constant, but he has fought his way to the top, and while he never planned on being a father, he will fight to make sure he has the chance to be a good one.

But the rules of the fight soon change and they both end up fighting the idea of love.

I hope you enjoy discovering whether love wins out!

Nina x

Consequence of Their Dubai Night

Nina Milne

Recycling programs
for this product may
not exist in your area.

ISBN-13: 978-1-335-73698-7

Consequence of Their Dubai Night

Copyright © 2023 by Nina Milne

For questions and comments about the quality of this book, please contact us at CustomerService@Harlequin.com.

Harlequin Enterprises ULC
22 Adelaide St. West, 41st Floor
Toronto, Ontario M5H 4E3, Canada
www.Harlequin.com

Printed in U.S.A.

Nina Milne has always dreamed of writing for Harlequin Romance—ever since she played libraries with her mother's stacks of Harlequin romances as a child. On her way to this dream, Nina acquired an English degree, a hero of her own, three gorgeous children and—somehow!—an accountancy qualification. She lives in Brighton and has filled her house with stacks of books—her very own *real* library.

Books by Nina Milne

Harlequin Romance

The Casseveti Inheritance

Italian Escape with the CEO
Whisked Away by the Italian Tycoon
The Secret Casseveti Baby

A Crown by Christmas

Their Christmas Royal Wedding

Hired Girlfriend, Pregnant Fiancée?
Whisked Away by Her Millionaire Boss
Baby on the Tycoon's Doorstep
Second Chance in Sri Lanka
Falling for His Stand-In Fiancée

Visit the Author Profile page
at Harlequin.com for more titles.

To Rosalind, my wonderful, all-singing, all-dancing
mother-in-law. With love. xx

Praise for
Nina Milne

CHAPTER ONE

MAX SAT ON the rooftop bar of the five-star hotel and looked out at the extravagant vastness of the Dubai skyline. The sheer size and scope of the architecture, the buildings that loomed and spiked and curved towards the night sky in an opulent dazzle of light caught his breath and for a moment at least distracted him from his thoughts.

Thoughts that he had held at bay all day as he focused on his packed schedule of business meetings, his intent to open an office here significantly advanced. His streaming platform already had a growing audience in Dubai and after today he had a much better understanding of what to offer. Satisfaction rippled through him—today marked another step forward for his company, another step that was taking it inexorably to global success. A quote from a recent article ran through his mind.

InScreen, the entertainment business founded by the charismatic Max Durante, is one of the hottest companies in the world, smashing analysts' growth predictions this year.

But not even the knowledge that his ambitions were being realised could edge out the emotions brought about by the letter he'd received three days ago, the words etched in his mind, running on a background repeat loop.

Dear Max,
I am delighted to inform you that we believe we have made progress in the search for your mother and we believe she may well be living in Mumbai.
    As you appreciate, Mumbai is a large city but we will endeavour to continue in our search.

Not for the first time he wondered what he would actually do if the detective agency did find his mother, the woman who had left him in a cardboard box as a newborn baby. Sometimes he brooded at the cliché of it, wondered where she got the box from, what had been in it before she packaged him into it and left him outside a London fast food restaurant.

Had she ordered something specially so that the box would fit a newborn baby? Or perhaps irony of irony it had been a parcel containing gifts? Or maybe she'd simply scoured the rubbish or recycling bins. It was one of the many questions that he'd considered time and again through his childhood.

Along with the perennial question of why. Why had she done it? Though deep down he knew why—his mother had been terrified he would be a chip off the old block. Bring her heartache and misery as his father had done before him.

Not that he had ever met his father either. But he knew about him. His uncle and aunt had turned up, unexpectedly, when Max was four, on the cusp of being adopted by the couple who had been fostering him. Even now he could recall the haze of confusion, punctured by the sharp, cold stab of understanding as his young self had realised what was happening. He could still remember the agonising sense of loss when he'd been taken from his foster parents, people who he had seen as parents, had been bonded to, had loved.

But love had counted for nothing—the long, cold arm of the law dictated that it was better for Max to go to 'real' family—blood had won out.

Which was ironic really.

Because his uncle, his father's older brother, believed in blood all right. Believed that Max was tainted with bad blood, that his veins ran with the same contamination as his father's before him. Max's father, Tommy, had been a charming bastard of the first order. A womaniser, a gambler, a cheat and a criminal who had died in a prison brawl. Max was shown photographs, the evidence all there that he looked uncannily like his father—perhaps his mother had seen that in those few hours she'd spent with him. Perhaps that's why nothing could change the mind of his uncle and aunt, their utter conviction of his inherent 'badness'.

He shook the thoughts away. There was nothing he could do to change his genetic programming—he was stuck with the face that looked back at him in the mirror every morning, the constant reminder of his origins.

But just because he looked like his father didn't mean he had to be like him. He had to believe that. Had to believe that his uncle and aunt had been wrong—that he was worth something. Hell in cold, hard cash terms he had a net worth of billions, but everyone knows money doesn't equate to goodness. His aunt had told him that in their final letter to him, when he'd been on the cusp of success, still hoping to win their approval. But it wasn't to be. Soon after they had died in a car accident and any small chance of redemption in their eyes was gone.

But Max was still proud of what he had achieved.

Hopefully one day his mother would be too.

Perhaps she already knew. In the numerous interviews he did, he'd made no secret of his start in life, made it clear he was open to contact…but so far nada; his mother had chosen to remain unknown.

A movement caught his eye, a flash of colour and he turned his head. A woman had entered the rooftop bar, a woman who looked vaguely familiar though he had no idea why. He'd certainly never met her because he knew he'd remember that. It wasn't just her looks, though it was impossible not to notice the ripple of corn-blonde hair, that shone in a waterfall of waves past her shoulders; to not clock the dress, black with a sweetheart neckline and a pretty print pattern of leaves, cinched at the waist with a patent leather belt. The outfit completed with white high heels that added height to a woman already tall, the effect designed to showcase a figure that combined curves and slenderness.

But she—whoever she was—had more than looks combined with a designer dress— this woman had presence and he'd swear she knew damn well that every eye in the room, male and female, was on her. It was an entrance and one he applauded, though he had no intention of doing anything about it. For a fleeting instant her eyes rested on him and he looked away, hoped that the grand arrival hadn't been staged for his benefit. It wouldn't be the first time he'd been accosted by a wannabe actress or producer, director...

He returned his gaze to the skyline and yet it was harder than it should be to not look round to watch her. A moment later he heard the sound of a raised voice behind him, and now he did turn and saw a man approach his...no not his...*the* mystery woman as she walked towards a table. He saw her halt, saw that she'd been shocked, a jerky awkwardness invaded the exquisite grace of her movements. Then an attempt at a smile that couldn't belie the tension in her body, one that increased as a petite dark-haired woman rose from the table and came to join them.

Was it his imagination or did the woman swivel almost as though she was contemplating making a run for it? Again her gaze rested on his and this time it was too late for him to turn away. The dark-haired woman spoke and although he couldn't hear her actual words he could hear the shrill tone, saw how tightly she now gripped the man's arm. For a mad instant he considered rising and going to the rescue, stopped himself. Mystery woman looked perfectly capable of rescuing herself and anyway who was to say she deserved saving? Resolutely he turned away once again.

But then a few seconds later he heard a voice, clear, melodious, well modulated. 'Would you mind if I join you? It would be most helpful to me and I promise it's only temporary.'

Stella Morrison put on her best smile as she asked the question, studied the man's expression as he raised his eyebrows, clearly considering his answer. Great! In truth she hadn't expected anything other than an instant agreement; in fact she'd anticipated enthusiasm.

In her experience most men were usually more than happy to be accosted by an attractive woman. Though she supposed a man like Max Durante might not be quite such a pushover as all that and yet…she'd seen his eyes rest on her for just a fraction too long as she'd walked in. Plus she'd known he'd watched her encounter with Lawrence and Juno, an unexpected meeting that still had her gut churning in sheer shock, as the past had waylaid her. But she could take pride in the fact none of that turmoil had shown on her face a few minutes before or now.

One of her many talents, along with an ability to read the room, to instinctively know who was who and what to say. But it seemed as though her usual instincts were skewed because she'd been sure she'd seen Max Durante make the smallest of movements earlier, as though he wanted to rise and come to her aid. But right now it looked as though she'd read this man wrong.

So she shrugged. 'Don't worry. Sorry to have bothered you.'

He emitted the smallest of sighs and then rose to his feet, moved round the table and pulled out a chair, with a somewhat theatrical flourish. 'I'd be delighted,' he said.

'Thank you.' She sat down, careful not to turn to look at her audience of two. 'I appreciate this and I'll keep it brief.' Summoning her best smile she added. 'Can I buy you a drink to say thank you?'

'Sure.'

A waiter materialised beside them and he looked up. 'I'll have a Macallan. On the rocks.'

'I'll have a Dance-off please.' Somehow the name suited the occasion; this was a dance-off situation, waltzing round Lawrence and Juno, about to embark on some sort of elaborate routine with the man sitting opposite her, studying her with a hint of wariness in his brown eyes. Though what he had to be wary of God only knew.

She returned the look, took her time as she assimilated his features, saw that in person Max Durante was even more compelling than he was on screen or in photographs. Dark, dark hair, tamed into a businesslike cut; eyes the colour of expensive chocolate surveyed her with a coolness she wasn't used to; chiselled features and a jaw that spoke of determination. His whole stance relaxed and yet she had the feeling his reactions were honed, that he was ready to face whatever the world threw at him. A body that must be partly due to time spent in the gym, the musculature defined without being overtly obvious, his body emanated a sense of power and entirely against her will she felt a frisson of pure desire run through her.

'So what is it you want from me?' he asked, his voice even, the words infused with an elaborate politeness.

Your body. She bit the words back, appalled at how nearly they had fallen from her lips.

Whoa, Stella. Get a grip.

This was not the time or the place—not when she was about to embark on a relationship. More than a relationship. A marriage. *If* all went to plan. And it would, because she was good at planning. And flirting with this man, any man, was not part of that plan. So 'your body' was not an option as an answer.

Instead, 'I want exactly what you've given me,' she replied. 'The chance to sit here long enough to make it look as though we agreed to meet for a drink.'

As if on cue their drinks arrived and she took a sip of her cocktail, welcomed the tang of tequila and lemon juice, diluted by tonic water and sweetened by the hibiscus foam. Saw the scepticism in his eyes and frowned. 'What do you think I want?'

A shrug, and her gaze watched the movement of his broad shoulders and tried not to be distracted. 'An opportunity to act? A promise of a meeting with a director? An invitation to some star-studded award.'

Huh. The frisson of awareness took a welcome morph into anger. 'So you think I'm stalking you? That I planned this.'

'Possibly. Or you may have seen an opportunity and you're taking it. Nothing wrong with that. I admire opportunism, but as a rule I don't reward it.'

'Then why did you agree to let me sit down and buy you a drink?' she flashed back. 'For the pleasure of saying no?'

'I agreed on the off chance you're telling the truth. You looked genuinely shocked to see the man who accosted you. Though of course you could be an excellent actress.'

So he had been watching her, and was observant enough to have spotted something she thought she'd successfully hidden. 'I wasn't acting. Or if I was I was trying to look as though I *wasn't* shocked. And for the record I am not interested in acting, or meeting a director and I am quite capable of scoring an invitation to a glamorous event without your help, thank you very much.'

There was a pause and then to her surprise he smiled. A real smile. Which warmed up his brown eyes and caused her gaze to linger on the firm line of his mouth. 'Glad to hear it,' he said. 'So all you need from me is table space and to look as though this is a what? A date?'

A date. The idea sent a strange tremor running through her even as she told herself that he wasn't suggesting a real date. And if he did she would refuse. Because she was strictly unavailable. On the verge of negotiating a marriage of convenience with Rob, Viscount Rochester, heir to the Earldom of Darrow. A marriage that would secure the future of her home; because once she had a son her ancestral home would be safe. Her son would be able to inherit the title and one day be Lord Salvington. Failing that Salvington would be lost, inherited instead by some distant male relative who had no interest in it.

And she wouldn't let that happen. Neither

for herself or for her sister. At the thought of Adriana guilt twanged inside her, strengthened her determination. Their father had never forgiven his younger daughter for not being the son he craved, the son he needed to be heir to Salvington. And so he treated her like dirt, put her down at any opportunity whilst he treated Stella like a princess. Stella had hated it, but she'd done nothing about it. Because any attempt to be kind to Adriana simply triggered her father's anger, an anger he took out on Adriana and their mother.

So Stella had allowed herself to be favoured, hell she'd reaped all the rewards with a vengeance, the generous allowance, the place in society, the parties, the balls. But through it all she lived with the constant drip feed of guilt, only alleviated by her determination to make it up to Adriana.

So the least she could do for her sister was save the home she loved. Plus it was hardly a sacrifice—Stella was fully on board with the idea of a marriage of convenience, had honed her persona to ensure she was perfect countess material.

But that was the future. At this point she and Rob hadn't even started discussions; had only agreed in principle that the idea was one they wanted to pursue when he returned from the States in two weeks' time. So technically she owed him nothing; but a real date was not an option, would be a pointless exercise.

But the idea of a fake date held a definite appeal. Because it was exactly what Lawrence and Juno needed to see. And… prompted an inner voice…this was her last chance to sit and maybe share some banter, flirt a little, enjoy the company of a gorgeous man.

'If you don't mind, that would be perfect.'

He raised his eyebrows. 'I'll think about it, but only if you explain why you need a fake date.'

Stella focused on keeping her expression neutral 'It's complicated.' Though in truth it was a lot worse than complicated and guilt surged through her very veins, all ideas of flirting legged it over the horizon as her mind reverted to years before, led her down a shadowed memory lane. 'Lawrence, the man I was speaking with, is an ex-boyfriend of mine.'

Lawrence Tenant had been part of a wild crowd, exactly the sort of boyfriend eighteen-year-old Stella had been looking for. All she'd wanted back then was to rebel, show her father how deeply angry she was with him. Because he had betrayed her, betrayed them all, by embarking on an affair in a deliberate effort to get another woman pregnant, in a bid to get a son. If successful her father would have abandoned them without hesitation.

So she'd rebelled, decided to hit the headlines in her own right. And Lawrence had been the perfect accessory—she'd reeled him in as she knew, oh, so well, how to do. A disastrous decision that kick-started a series of even worse choices until a denouement that had ended in near tragedy. All her fault.

But she hadn't seen Lawrence for years until tonight. And when Lawrence had risen and greeted her, she, supercool Stella Morrison, had panicked. Spooked by the wave of guilt and shame, spooked too by the shock in Lawrence's eyes. And so she'd come up with her plan, said she had to rush as she was meeting Max Durante for a drink.

Now to convince Max Durante of the same. 'It was a complicated break-up,' she said. 'And Lawrence is now happily married to the woman he is here with and…'

'His wife still sees you as a threat.'

'Yes.' Stella had heard a few years ago that Lawrence had married Juno, another girl in their group, and she'd been pleased, hoped it drew a line under the horror of the past. But today she'd seen fear, had instinctively understood that Juno was scared that seeing Stella would trigger Lawrence in some way. 'Which I'm not. But I wanted to show them that, wanted to avoid a scene.' Most of all she didn't want anyone to get hurt. 'So I said that I was here to meet you for a drink.' The words had fallen from her lips without a thought.

And she'd been sure it would work. Because she'd sensed Max's interest, and let's face it, whilst he'd been checking her out she'd been returning the favour. She'd seen him the moment she'd stepped onto the rooftop bar, sitting silhouetted in the expert lighting and something had caught at her.

'So what do you think?'

CHAPTER TWO

Stella tried not to hold her breath as she waited for his answer; he gave a quick glance behind her, managing to make it look as though he were looking for the waiter. 'Can you see them?' she asked.

'Yes. The woman is holding the man's hand and is talking. He looks a bit agitated.' He drummed his fingers on the table and then nodded. 'OK. Let's do it.' He sipped his drink. 'If we're on a date I'd better know your name,' he said.

'Stella. Stella Morrison.'

His brown eyes narrowed slightly and she could see him search his memory banks. 'Got you. High society. Aristocrat. Daughter of Lord Salvington. Few years ago you were in the papers a bit.'

'I didn't have you down as someone who follows the gossip columns.'

'Then you'd be wrong. I follow all news and trends as much as I can—it helps me work out the next best thing for InScreen. Plus I have an excellent memory. So I also know you haven't been snapped much recently apart from the usual, X attended the X ball blah blah.'

'I went through a bit of a phase a few years ago.'

A phase that had come to an end after the Lawrence fiasco. That particular scandal hadn't hit the papers, had been relegated to a few short paragraphs with her name kept out of it. In part, she knew, because her father had pulled some strings, but also because a far more newsworthy royal scandal had fortuitously struck. And Stella had been so guilt-stricken, so horrified by the consequences of her actions that she'd pulled back, returned to the 'perfect Stella persona'.

'Anyway,' she said. 'That's my name and obviously I already know yours.'

'So how did we meet to arrange this date?' he asked.

'Hmm. Let's see. Are you in Dubai on business or pleasure?'

'Business. What about you?'

'Pleasure.'

He looked around. 'On your own?' he asked and now his voice drew out the words.

'Nope.'

'You've come with your invisible friends?' he asked, deadpan and surprised a laugh out of her.

'No. They are real friends, but due to a flight cancellation they won't get here till tomorrow. So today I'm flying solo. Or I was anyway.'

'Well perhaps we bumped into each other at the airport and got a taxi here together and agreed to meet for a drink.'

'I think that's a bit dull,' she declared. 'If we're going to have a fake date I think we should give it some pizzazz.'

'OK. Go for it. How did we meet?'

'How about I saw you at your business lunch, waiting for whoever you were meeting.' She narrowed her eyes, pictured the scene. 'I'm sitting at the bar, sipping a... champagne cocktail and our eyes meet across the room and I decide to do something I'd never done before. I get a glass of champagne sent across to you...no not champagne a Hey Sugar cocktail or a passion fruit martini and a note with my phone number on it. You lift your glass in a toast and text me immediately and we end up arranging to meet for a drink here. What do you think?'

For a moment she could almost believe that was how it had played out and then he shook his head. 'Definitely wins in the pizzazz department, but it doesn't hold up.'

'Why not?'

'For a start it's stretching coincidence that we are both staying in the same hotel and ended up in the same restaurant for lunch.'

She waved a hand. 'Fate—it was fate not coincidence.'

'Plus I wouldn't have texted you.'

Stella blinked; this was a novelty she conceded. She was so used to men falling in with what she wanted, so used to being sure that rejection was not an option. 'Ouch.'

'Don't take it personally,' he said cheerfully. 'I wouldn't have texted any woman. I would have assumed you had an ulterior motive.'

'Fine. I was after a bit of pizzazz not realism. This is an imaginary scenario remember? So let's *imagine* that I sent across a Between the Sheets cocktail with a signed affidavit saying all I was after was your body and nothing else.' *Huh?* That was not what she had meant to say at all, and from the amused glint in his eye he knew it.

'OK. I like it. Impressive knowledge of cocktails and direct and to the point. Strong on pizzazz, but perhaps slightly lacking in the romance department.'

'I felt your somewhat pedantic approach meant romance isn't your thing.' Stella suppressed an inward sigh—so much for sophisticated banter. Calling an uber-successful, gorgeous man like Max Durante pedantic? Really?

'Romance may not be my forte, but let's say I have other strengths and talents I can bring to the…table. Or—' and now he wiggled his eyebrows '—any other item of furniture you care to imagine.'

His words surprised another laugh from her, but also caused heat to touch her cheeks as a sudden vivid image of what those talents might be rushed into her mind. And when she met his gaze she saw that amusement had faded from his expression, instead his gaze had darkened and awareness suddenly shimmered in the air. Forcing herself to blink and look away she picked her drink up, saw that her fingers were trembling as she took another sip. Realised too that her brain had fuzzed and for once she was struggling to find the right thing to say.

'A table works for me.' She replayed her own words and bit back a groan. That was not what she meant to say at all. 'For another drink,' she added desperately, knew she was making little sense.

'Or…perhaps we should have dinner?' he suggested. 'Use the table that way.' He raised a hand. 'And I promise not to mention the word *table* again.'

The glint of amusement was back in his brown eyes now, accompanied by a slight up-turn of his lips. Once again her gaze settled on the firm line of his mouth, once again her thought processes scrambled. 'Dinner?' she said.

'Yup. The meal you eat in the evening?' The teasing note shivered over her skin. Time to pull herself together.

'I know what dinner is,' she said tartly. 'I'm just not sure it's a good idea.'

'Why not?' he asked bluntly. 'We're both here alone, we both need to eat, and this is meant to be a date.'

Oh, Lord. Guilt jabbed at her; she'd been so distracted by Max that she'd actually for-gotten about Lawrence and Juno. What sort of person did that make her? But dinner? 'I…' *I'm very attracted to you and am worried I may succumb to temptation and proposition you*, whilst being true didn't feel like the right thing to say. 'I'm very nearly in a serious relationship,' she said instead. And she didn't want to send the wrong message— wasn't sure what message she wanted to send at all.

An odd expression crossed his face. 'I'm intrigued. Because coincidentally so am I.'

Now she raised her eyebrows. 'I thought you didn't believe in coincidence.'

He tipped his palms up in acknowledgement of defeat. 'Then perhaps it's fate.' He leant back in his chair. 'A sign. So how about we have dinner, no hidden agenda. Then we go our separate ways to our nearly serious relationships. That way your ex and his wife will also think our supposed date is going well. And I'm hungry.'

The prosaic words decided her. 'In that case dinner sounds good. Apparently the menu is to die for.'

Max studied the menu, made a decision and glanced across at Stella who was still looking down at the choices. What the hell was he playing at? OK he believed Stella's story about the ex-boyfriend, though he suspected there was more to it than she was admitting. But that was none of his business.

There had been no need to prolong this fake date—yet he had.

Why? Because…because he was enjoying himself—Stella intrigued him and then of course there was the attraction—no point in denial, the attraction so strong he was surprised their table wasn't surrounded by sparks.

But it was an attraction he had no intention of acting on; if she was with someone else then she was off-limits. No way would he try and persuade a woman to be unfaithful and no way would he step on someone else's turf. He would not follow in even one of his father's footsteps and apparently Tommy Durante had been a womaniser extraordinaire. But Stella hadn't said she was in a relationship, she'd said she was 'nearly' in one. A mirror of his own situation? In which case the moral high ground took on a different hue.

His thoughts went to Dora. Dora Fitzgerald, prospective heiress, a woman who had proposed marriage to him—a marriage on paper only…a marriage made purely for business reasons. A simple deal. She needed to be married to inherit the family business. He wanted to buy the family business. She wanted to sell the family business. The answer was obvious. A no-brainer surely. Dora's words. Yet he wasn't sure and so they were both thinking about it, in pre-negotiation stages. At this stage in proceedings he and Dora were free agents.

The waiter arrived with place settings, cutlery and a complimentary platter of food.

'Are you ready to order?' he enquired.

Stella smiled up at him. 'Could we have a few more minutes please?'

Max raised his eyebrows. 'You've read it at least three times,' he observed.

'Yup.' Stella smiled at him. 'This is an amazing menu. I love Japanese food and this isn't a real date.'

'Why does that matter?'

'Well, if it was a real date I might worry that you would get bored whilst I took ages to choose. Or I might think it's better not to order something messy. Or anything that might get stuck in my teeth. Especially if someone might catch it on camera.'

Max blinked. 'For real? You would think about all those things.'

'Of course. I'd be mortified if I got caught on camera with spinach in my teeth. Or got snapped with my date looking bored. So this is my last chance to take my time and order whatever I want.'

He opened his mouth and closed it again as she returned her attention to the menu, her head tipped to one side, a small frown on her face as she muttered under her breath.

The waiter returned and Stella smiled up at him. 'Thank you. I think I'm ready now. Please can I have the *nasu dengaku*, the *kitsune udon, the maguro* avocado *namaharumaki* salad, the *hirame* sushi and the spider roll and the *ika* butter *yaki*. Oh, and a glass of the sauvignon blanc, please.'

'I'll have the chef's selection of sushi and a glass of sauvignon blanc as well.'

Once the waiter was gone Stella stared at him. 'Did you even read the menu?'

'I skim read it, but I know I like sushi and I am sure the chef knows what he or she is doing.' He smiled at her. 'Oh, and I didn't want you to be bored whilst I chose.'

'Ha Ha!'

'But seriously if this was a real date you would have ordered differently?'

'Sure. I'd have been worried about the noodles falling off my fork, or the sauce dripping on my dress or…there are a lot of things to think about. Especially if I have journalists set up watching me.'

'So you want to be snapped?' he asked.

'Not normally, but if I am going to be I'd rather be in control of it and my next dates, well yes I plan for them to be in the public domain.'

'So this is your "nearly a relationship"?'

'Yes.'

'But it's not a relationship yet?'

'No.'

'But you don't want to tell me any more about it?'

'Would you tell me about yours?'

'I don't know,' he said honestly. 'It's confidential.'

She shrugged. 'So is mine. So we'd have to work on an "I'll show you mine if you show me yours" basis.' There was an infinitesimal pause and as their gazes met he saw her pupils darken, knew she was regretting the choice of words. 'That way we'd both have a hold over each other,' she finished smoothly.

'So much for trust,' he said.

'We'd be fools to trust each other. We've only just met.'

'Yet we're considering confiding in each other.'

'At minimal risk.' They paused as the waiter returned.

The risk would be minimal, but why take the risk at all? This business deal was massively important to him. Why take any chance of jeopardising it? Because dammit sometimes life was worth a little risk and he *wanted* to know Stella's story. Part curiosity, part welcome distraction from his own thoughts, and the knowledge that soon his mother might be found. Part—if Stella was a free agent then it changed the dynamics of their 'date' opened up a possibility of allowing the haze of attraction to gain a foothold.

And so, 'Deal,' he said and made to hold a hand out to shake on the deal, realised that that was hardly a 'date-like' thing to do and turned the gesture into something else. Covered her hand in his own. And felt it jump under his at the touch; her eyes shot to his face and he saw shock and surprise in the blue depths. Knew the same emotions were mirrored in his own eyes—because the touch had triggered something, a desire, a need to explore the attraction further, and had created a shimmer of awareness.

Whoa. The sheer intensity of his…their reaction shocked him and perhaps she thought the same as she gently pulled her hand away and then looked down at it, her blue eyes wide and now full of sheer desire. Before they both heralded the arrival of the waiter with relief.

Five minutes later Stella surveyed her side of the table. 'Hmm, perhaps I overordered a bit. You may need to help me out a little.'

'OK. I'll admit I was intrigued by the spider roll.'

'Crab and avocado rolled in seaweed. Then this—' she pointed, as she explained '—is the *nasu dengaku*, which is deep-fried aubergine with miso and sesame seeds, and the salad is rice paper roll with raw tuna and avocado and then there are the noodles—*kitsune udon* in a hot soup with deep-fried bean curd.' Her smile was broad with delight. 'We can slurp together.' She raised her glass. 'To fake dates,' she said softly.

He clinked his glass against hers. 'To this fake date.'

For a while they focused on eating and then, 'Right. Who goes first?' he asked.

'How about we toss for it?'

'The old-fashioned way? I'm in. Provided you have a coin.'

'I do.' She reached down into her bag and took out a small purse and tugged out a coin. 'Heads or tails.'

'Tails.'

She spun the coin up into the air and they both watched its descent into the palm of her hand. She flipped it onto the back of her hand. 'Tails it is. You win.'

'Then you go first,' he said.

She thought and then, 'I'll try to keep the background brief. My family live on the Salvington Estate. It has been in the Morrison family for generations, passed from son to son. However, my parents had two daughters, myself and my younger sister, Adriana. So no son. Which means the current heir is a distant relative who has no interest in the estate and would sell it off to the highest bidder. Unless I have a son, whilst my father is still alive. So the idea has always been that I would make a "grand alliance" and save the estate and that in a nutshell is exactly what I am planning to do. Marry a fellow aristocrat. Have an heir. I'll mix in high society,

I'll have money, status; and provided I have a son I'll save Salvington.'

'Is this aristocrat someone you know?'

'Yes. Well, I mean I don't really know him, but when we were younger we went to the same parties and he is a decent sort of bloke.' Max eyed her for a moment.

'I may not be the most romantic of men but I'm not sure "decent sort of bloke" is how I'd want my bride to describe me.'

Stella frowned. 'I don't think he'd mind. We both know this is a marriage of convenience. He is marrying because he needs an heir, and he wants the right sort of wife, who will be a good countess. I will be.'

He could hear the determination in her voice. 'You must love your family estate very much.' For a moment he tried to imagine what it would feel like to know your parents and all the generations before them, to be so rooted in your family history, to have a family tree, a place that was truly home. Rather than a cardboard box.

As he studied her face he saw a shadow cross her eyes and her voice seemed strangely flat as she said, 'Yes I do.' She nodded as if to emphasise the point. For herself or him he wondered. 'I love my home very much. But it is hardly a sacrifice on my part. I'll have money, status, position, an amazing home… and lifelong security.'

'But what about love?'

'Not interested.' Her voice was absolute and he wondered at the certainty. Decided not to question it; after all he didn't believe in love either. Or at least not for himself.

But… Max hesitated; knew this was nothing to do with him, yet… 'Well, what about attraction? I mean it's great that you think you'll like this guy, but you need attraction, a spark.'

Her blue eyes met his straight on and then she shrugged. 'He's a good-looking man, and I've been told that I'm a beautiful woman— I'm sure we'll manage.'

Max stared at her. 'It's not about being generically attractive. It doesn't work like that.'

'Of course it does.' She cast him a quizzical look. 'Are you saying you think he'll have difficulties managing?'

Max closed his eyes. 'No. I am quite sure he will understand the procedure and "manage" but surely you want more than just "managing".'

'Of course I do. But I am confident we'll work it out.'

An irrational surge of…what…jealousy, anger, frustration rippled through him. Along with sheer disbelief. How could she sit here with all the sparks leaping about between them and think it was OK to settle for managing.

'Really?' he rasped.

'Really. Plus attraction isn't the be all and end all is it?'

'No, but it's pretty important when you are proposing to spend your life with someone. When you last saw this guy was there even a flicker of attraction?'

'Well, no…but it was at least four years ago.'

'What happens if there still isn't a flicker.'

'We'll ignite one. How hard can it be?'

'I don't know. I've never tried to force an attraction that doesn't exist.'

'We'll work it out.'

'How? By rubbing two damp sticks together and hoping?'

'If need be.' Her eyes narrowed. 'I said we will work it out. Anyway I may set eyes on him and it will be instant lust. That can happen.'

His eyes lingered on her lips, dropped down to her hand, the one he'd covered scant minutes before. 'I know,' he said and she flushed.

'*Anyway*,' And there was a hint of gritted teeth about the word. 'That's my story. Your turn. I presume there are sparks galore in your nearly relationship?'

'No.'

She raised her eyebrows. 'So how does that work? I thought you said attraction was an important factor in relationships.'

'Usually it is critical to my relationships, but this is different. This time I'm contemplating marriage.' The very word caused unease to ripple through him, even as he hurried to explain. 'A temporary marriage, for business reasons only. My prospective bride needs a husband in order to gain her inheritance. Her inheritance includes ownership of a business I want to buy. So the marriage is strictly one of convenience, but we need to look the part and we need to remain married for two years. So it is not a lifetime commitment.'

She studied him. 'Yet you're clearly not convinced it's a good idea.' She gave a sudden small gurgle of laughter. 'You look like a man condemned. So why do it? Your business is already massively successful.'

'This deal would make it even more so.' Which was why doubts were redundant. Yet the idea of entanglement made him edgy, worried that even a marriage in name only would remove some of his precious autonomy.

'Then what's the problem? Two years isn't that long. And if the marriage is a paper one you won't be committed to anything.'

'Thank God.' Because he didn't want to be responsible for someone else's happiness. Because he wouldn't risk failure, a failure he knew would come. He wasn't relationship material, wouldn't risk being rejected, or worse rejecting someone; he knew how rejection felt; his mother had rejected him on sight, his foster carers had been forced to reject him, his uncle and aunt had rejected him with unassailable consistency. He'd had enough rejection to last a lifetime and he certainly wouldn't court any more.

'Then if commitment isn't your thing, which it clearly isn't, you have to work out if the business advantage is worth fake commitment.'

Max considered that. 'I suppose the problem is that even a fake commitment involves some real commitment, spending time together, making it look real, fidelity in the sense we wouldn't publicly humiliate the other. That is doable for two years, but you're planning to do that for your whole life.'

'No, I'm not,' she said. 'My commitment is real. I am planning on making a real commitment to a real marriage. And I plan on being happy.'

He couldn't hold back the snort of derision. Perhaps he was out of line, but somehow this conversation had got personal and the idea that Stella was about to give up on passion, the idea of Stella with a man who sounded duller than dishwater whatever his title and position, felt wrong.

'I take it you disagree.' And now her voice held icicles.

'Yup. A lifetime without a spark sounds… flat, dull, boring. However decent this man of yours is it can't compensate for passion, desire, the way a look can spark a shiver to run through your whole body.'

He couldn't help it now, wanted her to acknowledge that at least he had a point and so he looked at her, allowed how he felt to show in his eyes, let the desire, the passion show and saw the answer in her expression, the flush that heated her cheeks, the parting of her lips—and how he wanted to kiss her.

The temptation nigh on overwhelming. 'Like that,' he said.

She blinked, shook her head and turned to look out at the Dubai skyline. 'But where does "that" get me?'

'Where do you want it to get you?' he asked.

The question was so loaded Stella could almost feel the weight of it. Loaded with promise, and possibilities. Her brain fuzzed with a sense of awareness, her whole body still shivering from 'that' look. Her brain told her she should go, before she did something foolish and yet her body relaxed back onto the seat and she saw his eyes follow the movement, dark eyes holding a seriousness and a real question.

One she didn't have an answer to. When she'd sat at his table she'd thought she was in control; had sensed his interest in her and used that interest to get her what she needed. But two hours later and she no longer felt in charge; worse she didn't even care.

Because somehow their conversation had taken her to places she hadn't expected and when he'd spoken of a life without passion, a near bleak sense of regret had touched her. The regret not strong enough to turn her from her path but strong enough to urge her to…to what?

'What are the choices?' she asked softly.

'We drink our drinks, say goodbye and go our separate ways or we take this further. Provided I'm reading this right, provided you are feeling what I'm feeling.'

'Depends what you're feeling,' she said, in an attempt at lightness.

'Desire. Attraction. Need. An overwhelming temptation to lean over and kiss you.' He smiled and desire rippled through her at the molten heat in his voice. 'To play another version of "I'll show you yours if you show me mine".'

Now desire interlaced with warmth as she gave a small chuckle, then met his gaze full on. 'If we play that game this time you can go first.'

'It's your choice whether we play or whether we don't.'

She eyed him. 'I'm not changing my mind about my marriage plans.'

'That's your choice. I'm offering one magical night before we both go down our chosen paths. Whatever they may be.'

Magical—it felt exactly that, as if a spell had been cast, had preordained everything that had led to this moment. This choice. Her choice.

'Would it be magical?' she asked.

'Yes.' There was no doubt in his voice. 'I promise and I'm a man of my word.'

Stella looked out at the vast illuminations, the jut and curve of a landscape that had been built at such speed, from a desert to an urban spread, a monument to wealth and glamour, a hub of power and tourism, a place where she had chosen to come to mark one last weekend before she embarked on a journey that would last a lifetime.

There was that insidious sense of bleakness again and she shook it away. She wanted to marry Rob, she did. It was the right thing to do and the right life path, the right road for her to take. But here and now she wasn't yet on that road and it seemed to her that fate was giving her a chance to experience passion and she'd be a fool to turn it down. She would carry regret with her on the road and she didn't want that. Because right here and now she wanted the man sitting opposite her, wanted him with a yearn that almost scared her.

Met his gaze and saw his pupils darken to molten brown, knew on some visceral level that he wanted her as much as she wanted him and a shiver trembled through her tummy, a twist of desire so raw and pure and elemental that she gasped. Knew she couldn't walk away from 'that'.

She gave a small, shaky laugh. 'Your room or mine?'

CHAPTER THREE

'*YOUR ROOM OR MINE.*' The words echoed in her ears. Words that confirmed a decision she knew to be right. Yet she hesitated as it occurred to her that she didn't know this man, that desire could be leading her to danger. 'And I'm going to text a friend…telling her I'm on a date and I'll check in.'

He gestured with one hand. 'I have no problem with that and if there's anything else you want to do or want me to do to feel safe that's good with me.'

Her fingers trembled as she texted, sent the text, waited for Leila's quick reply.

Intrigued. Take care. Don't do anything I wouldn't do. Leaves you lot of leeway. LOL. Check in. I'll wait up.

Then, 'Let's go.'
In one lithe movement he rose to his feet,

moved round and pulled her chair out, the old-fashioned courtesy caught her off guard even as she caught her breath. The sheer proximity of him dizzied her and she forced herself to look casual, to look as though they were parting to go to their separate rooms. Forced herself to keep her walk slow and poised, even turned to see if Lawrence and Juno were still there, but they had already left and she hadn't even noticed.

They turned their backs on the skyline and headed to the door that led inside the plush hotel. The walk seemed interminable. Now that the decision was made every second where she wasn't exploring this attraction, this simmer of awareness seemed a waste. One night suddenly seemed infinitely short as anticipation swelled inside her, heightened with each decorous step. Then finally they were outside her room, in the thankfully otherwise deserted corridor.

Fingers trembling, she negotiated the lock and pushed the door open, somehow amazed that her room looked the same as when she left it, when she felt so changed. The king-sized bed, covered with the cool white duvet, the furnishings sleek and modern, a mixture of sand colours with lavender overtones.

The massive glass windows that showcased the Dubai skyline, the twinkle of hundreds of thousands of lights that illuminated the nightlife of so many different people. Her open suitcase in the corner, her make-up on the dressing table.

It seemed surreal that when she'd dressed just hours earlier, applied lip gloss, brushed her hair she had had no idea the evening would end like this. With this gorgeous, infinitely desirable man who had exerted such a power over her so quickly.

'Stella?' There was a hint of a question in his voice and she knew he was giving her a chance to back out.

Or perhaps he was having doubts. 'Max?' she replied, in the exact same tone.

This pulled a smile from him, a smile that seemed to warm her this time with a sense of reassurance that somehow intensified the desire, made her feel a sense of joy.

'Any doubts?' he asked, 'We can just sit on the balcony and have a cup of tea if you prefer.'

Now she smiled, a smile that turned into a gurgle of laughter. 'I thought you promised me magic?' she said.

'You've never tasted my tea,' he deadpanned back without missing a beat and now her laughter turned full-blown and somehow with that any awkwardness, any vestige of doubt disappeared and as the laughter subsided they closed the gap between them and she looked up at him.

'Maybe later,' she said. And then in what seemed like one fluid movement, where she couldn't tell who moved first she was in his arms and he was kissing her and she was kissing him. His lips evoked an intensity of pleasure so deep the need for more was almost painful. She could taste coffee and the sweetness of wine, felt his fingers tangle in her hair and he gasped as she pressed against him, wanting, needing more. He deepened the kiss and she slid her hand under his shirt, felt his reaction, the shudder of pleasure as she ran her fingers over the glorious muscular sculpting of his back.

As the kiss continued, and desire flared and sparked they were manoeuvring their bodies towards the bed. Once there, barely breaking apart, they tumbled backwards, hands greedily exploring, touching, feeling... every sensation pulsed and roared, every bit of her lost in this glorious whirl of passion. And so second after magical second, minutes, hours passed until finally satisfied they fell asleep in the early hours of the morning.

Eventually Stella awoke, opened her eyes and knew she was alone in the bed, felt an instant sense of bereft. Opened her eyes and saw that light infiltrated the room, highlighted the scattered trail of her clothes. And then she realised she wasn't alone, Max stood by the window, fully dressed and somehow that made her clothes look tawdry.

Now what? It seemed hypocritical to be embarrassed by her nakedness—after all she had slept naked in his arms, they had explored every millimetre of the other's body for hours. Her whole body still tingled from his touch, her fingers tingled with the sense of him, the scent of him. So she'd be damned if she would start trying to do contortions with sheets.

Instead she swung her legs out of bed, her back to him, rose and walked over to where the fluffy, luxurious complimentary bathrobe hung and pulled it on, tied it at the waist and moved towards him.

'Sorry to halt the great escape by waking up.' Even as she said the words she regretted them. 'Sorry. That was snide.'

'I wasn't escaping. I was waiting for you to

wake up so I could say goodbye. But it seemed wrong to stay in bed once I'd woken up and it seemed wrong to watch you sleep so...this was my solution. Coffee and the view.'

Goodbye. She knew there was no choice, knew too that she had no regrets. It was impossible to regret the previous hours, the joy, laughter, and sheer...passion, her body still felt alive, thrummed with remembered pleasure and for a mad moment she wanted to grab him by the shirttails and pull him back to the rumpled bed.

Knew in that instant that that was why he'd got up and dressed, because he knew temptation would be too much. The only way forward now was to say, 'Well I'm awake now. Thank you for staying to say goodbye. And thank you for last night—it was...'

'Incredible,' he said softly. 'I'm glad you chose my table and I wish you all the best with your future.'

'Ditto and likewise.' She stepped forward, wanted to be near him one last time. 'Goodbye Max.' As she stood on tiptoe she brushed her lips against his and moved hurriedly backwards, not wanting to make a fool of herself.

'Goodbye.' For a fraction of a second he

hesitated and then turned and walked to the door. She watched, waited until it clicked shut and then ran a hand over her lips and turned to the window.

She would not cry because that would be foolish—she wouldn't even be sure what she was crying for. Coffee and the view—that was the answer. Then her friends would arrive later in the day, then she would return to England and her real life and the future she had planned.

And she'd look back on Max as a pleasant interlude. No more, no less.

Two months later,
Salvington Estate, England

Stella stared down at the test result, closed her eyes and looked again. This could not be happening. This *could not* be happening. Only it was. The test had ninety-nine percent accuracy and more to the point she'd done it twice.

Fact: She was pregnant.

Fact: Max Durante was the father.

Fact: In an hour she was supposed to be meeting Rob, Viscount Rochester, for their first date, kick-starting a carefully planned, choreographed, all-singing, all-dancing schedule of dates, leading to an engagement announcement in a glossy celebrity magazine and culminating in a no holds barred high society wedding.

What was she going to do?

The question pummelled her brain as she paced the floor of her bedroom, one hand across her midriff. The sheer enormity of the knowledge so overwhelming she couldn't think beyond the one fact of her pregnancy. Having a baby. A baby, a tiny little piece of humanity with tiny fingers and toes.

But she couldn't… How could she have this baby? Baby. Baby. Baby. She and Max had created a baby. For a moment she was transported back to that magical night, a night she had tried not to dwell on, to keep in perspective, but now… They had used protection, so what had happened. Was it possible that one of those times, when he'd woken her in the early morning hours, half-asleep— could they have quite simply forgotten? Or perhaps there had been a faulty product or… What did it matter? She was pregnant.

Of course it was early days and she knew she had options, knew she didn't have to keep the baby. But…a fierce protective instinct unfurled inside her…she wanted to. Even though she could see how illogical it was, how it would mess up—no, wipe out—her entire life plan, she wanted to keep the baby.

So now what? She needed to talk to someone and who better than her sister, the one person who would grasp the magnitude of the issues at stake here. Because this baby would not be legitimate and therefore even if he were to be a boy he couldn't be the heir.

Stella left her room and headed towards the stairs, knew Adriana would be up in her study, located in the warren-like depths of the upper floor of Salvington Manor. Calling her sister's name she approached the door as Adriana pulled it open.

Stella frowned, saw a slight wariness in her sister's eyes and wondered why. Because although Adriana had every right to loathe Stella she didn't. Understood that it wasn't Stella's fault that she was the adored one, the apple of their father's eye. Understood, too, how much Stella hated that role.

'What's wrong?' Adriana glanced at her watch. 'And what are you doing here?' Her sister all too aware that she was supposed to be on her first date with Rob. A romantic lunch in one of Oxford's most expensive restaurants. Champagne and a discreetly alerted journalist in attendance.

'I can't go through with it.'

'Sorry?'

'You heard me.' Stella followed her sister into the study, resumed pacing, now in front of the battered mahogany desk.

'What do you mean? It's all arranged—you're the one who planned the whole thing.'

'I know. And I meant to do it, Ria, I really did. I wanted to do it.'

'I don't understand. What's happened? What's changed?'

Stella twisted her hands together. 'I'm pregnant.'

'What?' Shock conflated with confusion. 'But if you and Rob are…'

'It's not Rob's. He and I haven't even kissed.' Stella gave a strangled laugh. 'I had that planned for date number three in full view of the press. We were going to hold hands at date two. A peck on the cheek was scheduled for today—date one.'

'But…' Adriana's eyes widened. 'Then who is the father?'

'It doesn't matter.'

'Yes, it does. It matters a lot, given our situation. Are you going to marry him?'

Stella's strides increased. 'No. That is not an option.' Because Max was about to marry someone else, was a self-avowed commitment-phobe and they had a one-night deal. 'But neither is marrying Rob. I can't pretend the baby is his.'

Adriana studied her. 'But you thought about it? Is that why you've left it this late to pull out of this date?'

'I only did the test today. I know I should have done it before, but I thought… I hoped I would be wrong. I even thought if I were to be pregnant it wouldn't matter. I'd have an abortion. But now…' She rested her hand on her tummy. 'Now…now I know it's a disaster but I want to keep the baby.' She stopped. 'Please don't give me a hard time. I know I've messed up, messed up our whole plan, but I'll make it right somehow in the future…'

'Whoa. Slow down. I'm not going to give you a hard time—I would never do that. You're my sister and you've always been the best sister I could wish for. As for the plan, you don't need to worry about that right now. Because we have far bigger worries. If you don't go through with marrying Rob, Father is going to go ballistic.'

She could see the fear on her sister's face

and guilt panged inside her again. Adriana had lived her whole life in the shadow of that terror, had to listen to their father denigrate her and put her down all her life. And Stella— she should have stuck up for her sister more, but she hadn't. Had gone along with the idea that it was 'easier' to deflect her father's anger by trying to keep him happy whilst Adriana rendered herself as invisible as possible.

The coward's way out, but she'd salved her conscience with the idea that she would save Salvington and give her sister what she wanted most—a chance to run the estate, and now…now she wasn't even going to do that. That was far worse than any fear of her father.

'What are we going to do?' Adriana asked.

'I'll have to tell Father,' Stella said. 'And there's another problem. Rob will be in the restaurant by now.'

'You need to tell him. We can't leave him stranded.'

'I know.' Stella frowned, resumed pacing. 'The problem is, I've got press all lined up to catch us. I've dropped all the right hints and I'm pretty sure there will be at least one celebrity journalist in that restaurant to scoop us. So they will see him take my call, or get my text.' Her stride increased. 'I can't think straight. But if the press get even a glimmer of suspicion about my condition, then…'

'We are up the creek without a paddle or a stick.'

'More than you know. I can't risk the paternity of this baby coming out. I can't.' Stella's voice broke. 'But there is one thing we could do…'

'What?'

'You can go in my place.'

'No way. That is the most ridiculous idea I've heard.'

'I don't mean marry him, just go and fake this date. Explain the situation to Rob. I'm sure he'd prefer that then being publicly stood up.'

'But…'

Fifteen minutes later, Adriana was primed and ready to go. At least the restaurant was only a short journey away. Once she'd waved her sister off, Stella knew what she had to do next. Face her father; her nerves fluttered at the thought, but she comforted herself with the knowledge that Lord Salvington had never been truly angry with her, even when she'd wanted him to be. Even when she'd partied and caused scandal after scandal.

Bracing herself she headed towards the east wing of the manor where her parents' rooms were, knocked on her father's door and pushed it open.

He turned from his desk and rose to his feet, a frown gathered on his forehead.

'Shouldn't you be with Rob?'

'Yes, but… I'm not going. There's something I need to tell you. I'm pregnant.'

'With Rob's baby?'

'No. Someone else's. So I can't go through with marrying Rob. I'm going to keep the baby.'

'And marry his father?'

Deep breath and, 'No. That isn't an option. So…'

She didn't see it coming, so sure that he couldn't find fault with her that it took her brain a few vital seconds to absorb the change in his expression, to see the sheer rage that mottled his features.

'Isn't an option? Are you telling me that you are going to produce a bastard, instead of an heir to Salvington, that you have sullied our name, betrayed me and everything you stand for. How dare you?'

She stepped backwards as he advanced, thought that he was going to hit her. Instinctively she pulled her phone out of her pocket, flinched as he snatched it from her hand and threw it at the wall. Saw him gather himself together and as fear grabbed her he shouted, 'Get out—out of this room and out of this house and out of my sight.'

Stella turned and fled, ran downstairs and to her car, knew she could find sanctuary in a hotel room. And sanctuary was what she needed right now, somewhere where she could somehow try and get her head round the fact that her life was now irrevocably changed, the whole carefully planned and constructed house of cards had collapsed in a fluttering heap around her. She placed a hand on her tummy. 'Don't worry,' she whispered. 'I'll look after you.'

CHAPTER FOUR

A few weeks later

MAX DRUMMED HIS fingers on his desk as he studied his itinerary for his upcoming Mumbai trip.

He had an extremely lucrative business deal in the pipeline, and a number of meetings lined up with some key players including Bollywood producers and stars. But he also wanted to soak up the culture, wander round and…and what? Bump into his mother who would of course instantly recognise him and—and run a mile in the opposite direction no doubt.

The buzz of his phone was a welcome relief from his thoughts.

'Hey,' he said to his PA.

'Um… I've got a woman here, wanting to see you. Says you met her in Dubai and you agreed to a meeting next time she was in

London to discuss a reality show about first dates, but she isn't after an opportunity to act, a promise of a meeting with a director or an invitation to some star-studded award.' His PA sounded puzzled. 'Normally I'd tell her no one sees you without an appointment but oddly she sounds legit. She also looks familiar though it's hard to tell with the sunglasses, scarf routine. So I thought I'd check with you.'

Max stifled the sudden sense of shock, moved to shut down the stream of memories—memories he had held at bay for the past few months, refusing to access them, despite the ridiculous number of times Stella had popped into his head, only to be ruthlessly squashed down. He'd found himself scouring the papers for news of her impending nuptials, to see the first date hit the headlines. But nothing…and he'd wondered if perhaps she'd baulked at the idea of a passionless marriage after all. He'd hoped so, even found his hand hovering over the phone. But of course he hadn't called. There would be no point.

Especially when he had decided to go ahead with his own business marriage.

Perhaps he should refuse to see her, but

that would be rude. Stella must have some reason for being here. Only one way to find out. 'Send her in,' he said.

To his own irritation he could feel the thump of his heart against his ribs, as anticipation churned inside him. Then after a perfunctory knock, Mariella pushed the door open and ushered Stella in, nodded at Max and retreated.

He rose to his feet, actually glad that his desk separated them, gave him a barrier to absorb the impact of seeing her.

She tugged the scarf off her head and pushed the sunglasses atop her blonde hair in an impatient gesture and for a long moment they stood staring at each other. Stella looked different, every bit as beautiful, but there was something he couldn't put his finger on, a subtle change. Her blue eyes held a certain something he couldn't decipher, the gloss of her hair held an extra lustre. But what hadn't changed was the instant charge, the magnetic pull of attraction, the urge to take up where they left off.

Her blonde hair was pulled back and then caught in a clip, tendrils escaping to frame her face. Blue eyes studied his face, as if she too was drinking him in, eyes that were shadowed with a trepidation that had been absent in Dubai.

'Stella. This is unexpected.'

'Yes.' Her lips twisted up into a smile that held wryness. 'I saw the article about your first date.' The article had come out two days ago, started with 'Spotted in the Wild—CEO Max Durante and heiress Dora Fitzgerald. Is it a date? The notoriously single CEO of In-Screen certainly looked smitten as the possible couple...blah-blah'. 'And I'm not here to make trouble.'

'Then why are you here?' He saw her hands curl into fists as though she were digging her nails into her palms, saw her shoulders pull back as she took a step backwards as if in preparation to turn and run, and a sense of foreboding trickled through him.

'I'm pregnant.' There was a moment where the penny failed to drop where he could only look at her in bewilderment and she continued. 'With your baby.'

He rocked backwards and tried to steady himself, failed and reached out to grasp the edge of his desk. Every instinct scrambled, but it was terror that won out, topped the mix with a murky grey swirl. He couldn't be a father; couldn't...wouldn't. Shouldn't.

He was not dad material, it was a path he would never choose to take, would never take the risk that he would let a child down—the idea enough to make him go clammy. He could feel all colour drain from his face, as he stared at her; his gaze dropped to her midriff and a sense of awe touched him, tried to thread through the panic. A baby, his baby was growing inside Stella.

'I get it's a shock,' she said. 'And as I said I'm not here because I expect anything. I know that you have marriage plans, but I thought you should know. Had a right to know that you are going to be a dad, but I understand that you may not want to acknowledge the baby, but one day the baby will ask me who his or her dad is and...'

Her words cut through the electric chaos that was blindsiding his brain. He had spent his whole life wondering about the identity of a parent who had abandoned him, spent years piecing together information about a father who he wished wasn't his father. There was no way he would, could or should put any child through even a fraction of that.

'Look, I know it takes a bit of time to process.' She twisted her hands together. 'Perhaps if you can call me or something in a few days, or a week or well…however long it takes. I'll write my number down and wait to hear from you.' She moved over to the desk in search of pen and paper. Clearly in a rush to leave, as if she'd done her duty and now she was going to run.

The movement, her proximity, the ridiculously familiar floral scent jolted his vocal chords into action. 'No. Don't go.' There was too much he needed to know and an instinctive part of him did not want her to walk out with his baby. What if she didn't come back? A reversal abandonment. The idea acted like the equivalent of a bucket of ice to the head, cleaved through the pandemonium of his thoughts and allowed him to focus. 'We need to talk.'

'I know, but if you want a bit of time first, or need to talk to Dora, that's fine.'

'I'm about to fly to Mumbai on a two-week business trip.' A trip he did not want to cancel; there were too many meetings lined up, too many opportunities he might lose. But the thought of being that far away from Stella, of not knowing what she was doing was not possible. 'Come with me.'

'Excuse me?'

'Come with me,' he repeated.

Trepidation vanished from her eyes, re-placed by ire. 'Has it occurred to you that I might have commitments?'

The question sent a volt of unease through him. Just because there had been no publicity didn't mean she wasn't still considering marriage. Scenarios chased through his mind, a small private wedding, an engagement kept under wraps until she'd spoken with him. The very idea of his baby being brought up under another man's roof, by some boring, upper-class aristocrat, caused his hands to clench.

'Do you?' he asked, the syllables grinding past his teeth. 'Because if you do I will postpone mine.'

She hesitated, blue eyes narrowed and then shook her head. 'Why not wait until you come back?'

'Because I have just found out I am having a baby—months after the event. Why didn't you tell me straight away?'

'Because I wasn't sure what to do, whether to tell you at all. Then I saw the article and knew it was now or never, whether your marriage is a business deal or you are smitten I thought you both had a right to know.'

Whether to tell you at all. Now or *never*.

Anger roiled through him. 'So you really considered *never* telling me? Letting our child grow up without knowing who his father is?'

'Yes, I did.' Her chin tilted out defiantly. 'And if I had believed that was the best thing for my baby then I would have done it. But in the end I didn't. So I *am* here and I have told you.'

And she looked as though she was regretting it and fear threw an insidious dart that pierced him. Because if she decided to turn and walk away from him there was little he could do to stop her. The realisation set his whole being on edge with both fear and powerlessness. Which meant he needed to calm down and stay calm. Do what he did best—negotiate.

'Then let's move forward from here and decide what to do next. We need to talk and I don't want to wait. So either you come to Mumbai or I'll stay here.'

She bit her lip and despite everything his gaze snagged on her mouth, lingered there as memories cascaded back of kissing her, the sheer gloriousness of those lips.

'If I come to Mumbai with you it would generate publicity and I don't want that and

I'm assuming you and Dora don't either. Also surely you need time to discuss this with Dora?' She hesitated and then twisted slightly away, her voice studiedly even, though he saw her hands clench. 'Are you smitten? Did you lie to me in Dubai?'

'Excuse me?' Max blinked. 'No, I didn't lie. At all. I told you in Dubai that we needed to make the marriage look real so it wouldn't be challenged by the trustees. So that date was fake.' There was a silence and he remembered their fake date, the banter, the laughter, the simmering shimmer of mutual attraction, heightened and spun as the golden moments had gone by lit by the sprinkle of stars and the dazzling illumination of Dubai's night sky. 'Really fake,' he added. 'Orchestrated for the cameras.'

'OK.' Her gaze remained steady, but something flashed across her eyes, akin to relief. 'I'm glad you didn't lie. But Dora still needs to know.'

'I know that and I will talk with Dora.' He had no idea how Dora would react to this, but he knew that no matter what he would be there for his baby. That was the only thought that shone neon bright through the sheer panic generated by the thought of being a father. He had to be there. Whatever the cost, whatever the price. 'I'll speak with her before we leave for Mumbai.' He saw the raised eyebrow at his use of the pronoun and hurried on. 'I understand you don't want any speculation or publicity if you come to Mumbai, but there doesn't need to be. We can stick to what you told my PA. We met in Dubai, I said to look me up in London to discuss a business idea, here you are. I like the idea, I say come to Mumbai so we can discuss it further. I think it will cause more speculation if I cancel my trip and stay here and then we are spotted together.'

'Fair point. I'll come to Mumbai. The sooner I decide what to do next the better.'

Relief trumped all other emotions at her words. He had two weeks now, two weeks to cut an agreement. To make a deal that meant he would be part of this baby's life.

Stella pulled her suitcase behind her and wondered whether this was a complete and utter mistake. But…it beat what she'd been doing over the past weeks—sitting in friend's houses and then in a soulless hotel room staring at the walls, engulfed in guilt and doubts and worry and fear. Reliving the circumstances that had followed her disastrous encounter with her father. Reliving the phone call from Adriana that evening.

'Dad's in hospital. He's had a heart attack. I found him at the bottom of the stairs when I got back from the date.'

She'd stood there clutching the phone in her hand as the ramifications exploded in her brain. This was her responsibility, her bad... However complicated her relationship with her father, he was still her father. And now he was in a hospital bed because of her. She'd messed up...again.

Unbelievable.

And now, now she'd told Max about the baby— What if that was another bad decision? After all, what did she even know about him? Perhaps she should swivel round and make a run for it.

Too late; Max had seen her. And there it was—the rush of hormones. He looked gorgeous in dark blue jeans and a black top and the knowledge that she knew exactly what he looked like, felt like under the clothes gave her a shocking thrill, which she knew she had to suppress. Because that part of their relationship was over. That magic had created a baby, their baby and her priority now was that baby. She needed to assess how good a father Max would be and she couldn't let attraction cloud her judgement or fuzz her brain. Not now, not ever. Not with her history of disastrous decisions.

So after a quick check to make sure she wasn't drooling she stepped forward, tried to access her poised Stella persona, the one she seemed to have misplaced somewhere along the way.

'Hey,' she said, glad her sunglasses hid her expression from him.

'Hey. We need to check you in then let's fly.'

A seamless fifteen minutes later she boarded the private jet, looked round its luxurious trappings that made it feel as though she was aboard a flying hotel suite rather than a plane. 'Do you usually fly privately?'

'No, not always, more when circumstances dictate. I find it's a good place to conduct private meetings and today I figured utter privacy is better. We have a lot to talk about and here seems a good place to start.'

'Agreed. Where would you like to start?'

Not even a heartbeat of hesitation. 'With your aristocrat. I assume the marriage plans are off.' Stella opened her mouth to concur as he continued. 'Obviously you cannot marry him now.'

The phrase held arrogance and she bristled. If Max Durante thought he could call the shots he had another think coming. The very idea triggered memories of her own upbringing, where her father had held all the power and the rest of the family had danced to his tune. 'I can do whatever I want,' she said. 'If I decide to marry Rob, or anyone else for that matter, that is up to me. My choice and absolutely nothing to do with you.'

'It would be everything to do with me,' he growled and the deep rumble of his voice held further autocracy. Her eyes narrowed, but his glower didn't back down.

'And would you allow me to dictate your marriage choices. I haven't asked you not to marry Dora.'

'You don't have to ask me. I've made that decision myself.'

Oh. The statement wrong-footed her. 'Why?'

'Because it wouldn't be fair. To Dora. Or the baby. There will be publicity and it wouldn't be much fun for her to go through that. But it is more than that. In order to maintain our fictional marriage, Dora would need to spend time with the baby and then what happens after the divorce? If she has bonded to the baby and vice versa.'

Stella blinked. *She* should have thought of that, instead of trying to score cheap points. Yet she also knew she couldn't show weakness, couldn't let Max think he could dictate her actions. 'I'm sorry you've lost the business deal,' she said. 'But I agree it is the right decision for the baby's sake. But me marrying Rob is a different scenario. It would be a lifelong commitment. It would be good for the baby to bond with him as soon as possible.'

'So you are seriously considering it?' Each word said perfectly calmly, but each word could have cut steel.

'That isn't the point. The point is I have every right to consider it. And it has nothing to do with you.'

'Nothing?' His tone was low, full of incredulity. 'You think I should stand back and do nothing? Watch you marry someone else, see my baby be brought up by another man, with me in the background. A man who you don't even love and I don't even know. I don't know how he would behave towards another man's child. Do you still think this has nothing to do with me?'

She could hear the pain in his voice, under the anger, and she paused, as her own anger diluted; how would she feel if biology had dictated a reversal? If Max was keeping the baby and bringing her up with Dora and she, Stella, was relegated to seeing her own child less than Dora did. How would she feel even now if he married someone she didn't know, someone who would spend extensive time with her child? The idea sheened her with panic and the anger died as suddenly as it had flared, and instinctively she raised her hand and tentatively reached out to touch his arm. 'Sorry. I'm sorry. I didn't think.' Her besetting sin really; she didn't think and people got hurt. 'I am not marrying my aristocrat. I didn't go ahead with the plans. I shouldn't have let you think I was. I'm sorry.'

There was a silence and then he exhaled and the tension in his shoulders that she hadn't even noticed was there relaxed. 'I'm glad,' he said simply and she knew the pain he'd felt had been real, not a simple desire to dictate her actions. Then he covered her hand with his own and there it was, a sudden sense of warmth, like a switch turning on, the feel of his fingers around hers exerted a pull, a sense of togetherness, a reminder they had created this baby together. And that warmth morphed into something else akin to the first spark when a fire was lit. Her gaze fixed on his hand, the shape, the strength, the memory of his fingers on her body, the magic they had wrought and as that hand brushed against hers she bit back a mewling sound of need. She knew that despite everything she still craved his touch, her skin seemed to shiver in remembered response.

As awareness threatened to escalate further, he lifted his hand just as she moved to do the same.

'OK. Good. But right now I am not planning on marrying anyone.'

'OK. Good. And neither am I.'

She essayed a small tentative smile. 'Then we can cross an item off the agenda.' She resisted the urge to rub her hand where he'd touched it, that warmth still there. Whoa. Now she was completely overreacting to a simple gesture and it was time to change the dynamic before she ended up doing something foolish. Her current speciality it would seem.

But she could at least make an attempt to be normal, poised, *together* Stella. 'Speaking of agendas, I meant to give you this as soon as we took off. In case anyone does check up on our cover story, I prepared this.' She reached into her bag. 'It's a proposal for an aristocratic reality dating show.'

She handed him a folder and he reached across to take it. Careful, they couldn't afford even an accidental brush of the fingers and she snatched her hand back and watched as the papers fluttered to the ground.

'Sorry.'

For heaven's sake—what was wrong with her? where was her famed poise and cool now?

'Sorry,' she said again and leaned forward to pick the papers up as he did the same. 'Ouch.' A shot of pain jolted through her as their heads collided and she heard his sharp intake of breath.

She sat back up. 'Shit, I'm sorry. Again.' And to her horror she felt a tear trickle down her cheek.

Instantly he was on his feet and then squatting down in front of her. 'Are you Ok? Let me see.' Before she could stop him he had pushed her hair away from her face, and was running his hand over the hurt area. 'Is it there?'

She caught her breath at the gentle touch

of his fingers, swept back to that magical night. 'I—I'm fine. Really.' Wide-eyed she met his gaze, saw the concern in his dark eyes morph into something else and knew his thoughts had synced with hers. She gave a half laugh—then closed her eyes as to her horror another tear seeped out.

'You don't sound fine,' he said softly and there was genuine sympathy in his voice. But then he moved away only to return a couple of minutes later. 'Here you go. Tea and tissues.' And then with a small laugh in his voice, 'I told you my tea was magic, didn't I?'

She gave a half chuckle and picked up the steaming cup. 'Thank you and sorry. I'm not usually like this. Maybe it's hormones.'

'So what's wrong? Apart from a bumped head.'

'I… I feel…lost.' She tried to sound flippant. 'I seem to have misplaced the usual normal Stella. I mean I never cry, I certainly don't drop things and I don't then bump heads with people. And I…always know what I am doing. And now, since the pregnancy, since my father's heart attack… I have no idea about anything.'

'Whoa.' He leant forward now. 'I didn't know about the heart attack.'

She nodded, started to shred the tissue paper. 'I told him I was pregnant, told him I was backing out of the marriage and he lost it. I left and then a few hours later he had a heart attack.'

'And you blame yourself?'

'Of course I do.' However much both Adriana and her mother told her it wasn't her fault Stella couldn't help but believe it was. 'If only I'd broken the news better, if only I'd never met you, if only I hadn't agreed to one magical night. But then I wouldn't have the baby and I do want the baby and it's not the baby's fault and…my father won't even see me. And if he dies Salvington will be lost and we'll all be homeless and…' Oh, God, she was such a mess. Unable to access the cool, sophisticated persona she had spent so long cultivating.

'How is he?' Max asked.

She took a deep breath. 'He's stable, but it turns out he'd had a couple of minor heart attacks in the past so the prognosis is a bit rocky. But right now the doctors say he is unlikely to have another attack as long as he takes care.' Yet the guilt wouldn't recede, compounded by Adriana's decision to take her place and marry Rob. To save Salvington. So instead of making things up to Adriana, she'd pitchforked her into an arranged marriage.

'I'm sorry about your father and I am sorry that the news about our baby triggered his heart attack. But it is not your fault and it certainly isn't the baby's. He or she didn't ask to come into being.'

Stella sighed. 'But we didn't ask either did we? I mean I'm not even sure how it happened.'

Her gaze met his and the atmosphere changed as Stella recognised the fallacy of her words. She knew exactly how it had happened and for a moment she was transported back, to the tangle of sheets, the feel of his hands glissading over her skin, the sculpt of his back under her fingers, the slow languorous burgeoning escalation of pleasure, yielding to an urgency and desperation.

She lifted her hands to cover her cheeks, felt the heat and flush of remembered passion and stared at him wide-eyed. 'I—I mean… technically I know how it happened but…'

'But we were using protection. Or at least I thought we were. Perhaps one of the times, we didn't.'

The time they'd both woken up to find

themselves half asleep in each other's arms? She closed down the memory, knew it served no purpose to relive that night.

'Whatever happened, happened,' she said. 'And here we are.' She touched her tummy. 'I want this baby, I love this baby, but… I'm terrified.'

'That's normal. Your whole life has been upended, all your plans gone, your father is ill and you're about to become a parent for the first time and you've been carrying that alone. But now you don't have to anymore. You can share the terror with me. And we can make a new plan.'

'That sounds good.'

He held a hand out. 'Hand it over then.'

'Hand what over?' She looked at him in confusion and saw that he was studying her with a small smile of his lips.

'Half the terror.'

'Huh? How does that work?'

'Imagine it.' Now his face was serious, though his eyes also held a glint of humour at her expression. 'Imagine it. You told me in Dubai you had imagination so picture the terror. Maybe it is a big grey blob, maybe it's bright pink and wobbly with hundreds of legs. Picture it, halve it, hand it over.'

'You're serious.' She shrugged. 'I feel ridiculous but… OK.' Stella closed her eyes and pictured the terror, all the horrible feelings of confusion, guilt and panic that had assailed her over the past months, a misogynous blob, brown and sludgy interlaced with purple and red veins. Carefully she pictured halving it and handed over the imaginary mass to Max.

'I can't believe I'm saying this but that actually helped.' She looked at him, a small frown on her face. 'I also can't believe I am asking this but what are you going to do with it?'

'I'll get rid of it.'

'How?'

He shook his head with mock solemnity. 'Trade secret.'

'What trade? You're CEO of a global streaming platform.'

'Not that trade.'

'Which one?'

'Magician,' he said, and she laughed.

'So you offer tea and therapy.'

'Amongst other things.'

She gave a small intake of breath, knowing exactly what other things he was referring to.

'But it's probably best if we don't go there,'

he added. 'Especially in the context of what I am going to suggest as the next part of my therapy.'

'What's that?'

'Bed. Another perk of this jet is that over there is a seat that converts into a very comfortable bed.' A funny little tremor ran through her and she saw desire darken his eyes even as a rueful smile tipped his lips. Lips that had wreaked such glorious pleasure. 'So you can sleep. You look exhausted and that's hardly surprising. So sleep. We can come up with a plan once we're in Mumbai.'

Sleep. She tried to remember the last time she'd slept properly, without vague edgy dreams or waking up in the early hours of the morning to a jumble of thoughts that wouldn't be blocked out. 'Sleep actually sounds pretty good.' And as she lay down and rested her head on the silken plump softness of the pillow she realised that this was the first time in weeks she'd felt safe.

CHAPTER FIVE

MAX FOCUSED ON his computer screen, kept his gaze resolutely turned away from the corner of the jet where Stella still slept. Knew it would be intrinsically wrong to watch her whilst she slept, however much he wanted to watch over, to guard the woman who carried his baby.

Baby. The word seemed to scroll across the screen, erasing the rows of figures and projections on the spreadsheet. Each letter undulated with a panic he knew he had to suppress—how he wished he could soothe his own terrors with tea and sleep. But he had no idea how to extract the dark thoughts and fears. Because the baby existed and the baby was stuck with him, Max Durante, for a father. Nothing could change that. In the first throes of panic he'd actually wondered if it would be better if he simply bowed out, but he couldn't do it. Couldn't abandon his baby, repeat history; that would be unforgiveable, unjustifiable. The idea of facing that child one day, trying to make him or her see that he'd done it for the best made his skin go clammy.

Because he knew if he found his mother and that was the line she spun he would try to understand, but on a visceral bone-deep level he wouldn't get it, wouldn't understand why she hadn't tried, given him a chance. Given herself a chance.

But maybe she'd been the same as his uncle and aunt, so convinced badness was baked in, bred in the bone that she hadn't seen the point in giving him a chance. That was what his aunt had told him. *'Your mother, she must have seen it in your eyes.'*

The words in their simple cruelty had rung with truth. Enough. That was then, his mother had judged him, abandoned him, but that would not happen to his child.

His child would have a mother and a father.

He turned now to look at Stella, filled with a sense of gratitude that at least Stella wanted this baby. He might not know much about her, but he did know that. She opened her eyes, clouded with sleep and a hint of confusion that morphed into a memory of where she was and she sat up, a small frown on her face.

'Sorry,' he muttered. 'I promise I wasn't watching you. I was about to wake you up. We'll be landing soon.'

She sat up, swinging her long legs over, rising and moving with natural grace across to her seat where she strapped her seat belt on. 'I really needed that sleep. Thank you.' She looked out of the window. 'I've never been to Mumbai before.'

'The hotel isn't far from the airport. I called before we left—they said an extra room shouldn't be a problem.'

'Thank you and of course I'll reimburse you.'

'No need,' he said. 'If you were really a consultant I would pay your expenses.'

'But I'm not really a consultant.'

'I know, but as I am the one who insisted you come to Mumbai I think it is fair for me to pay.'

Was it his imagination or was there a soupçon of relief on her face as she considered his statement, then nodded. 'Thank you. I appreciate that.' Surely she couldn't be in money difficulties. Though why not; it occurred to him that in actual fact he knew absolutely nothing about the woman sitting opposite him. What was her job, what was her favourite colour? He had no idea. All he knew was that she was beautiful, that there was a magnetic pull of attraction between them and she was the mother of his baby.

Fear suddenly trickled in, cancelled out the warmth he'd felt earlier. Because if he didn't measure up, just as he hadn't for his mother, just as he hadn't for his aunt and uncle then Stella had the power to take his baby from him. Or force a custody battle, or refuse to put him on the birth certificate, or move to the Outer Hebrides, or poison his child against him. And God knew he knew how easy that was to do, his aunt and uncle had dripped negativity into his very soul.

Whoa. There was no need to believe she would do any of that, but he shouldn't forget that she could.

'Max?'

He blinked and turned to Stella. 'Are you OK?'

'I'm fine,' he said as the wheels hit the runway. It would be fine; he'd do whatever it took to make it fine.

Half an hour later Max watched as streets flashed past as the driver expertly navigated the traffic-clogged roads of Mumbai, looked out at the crowds of humanity that jostled each other, looked at the streets lined with stalls and shop fronts, people and livestock. Was his mother one of those people, passed by in a flash, in the overwhelm of people, the plethora of scents and smells that assaulted his senses, the cacophony of noise.

The car pulled up outside the imposing exterior of the hotel and after thanking the driver they climbed out, blinked in the sunshine and felt the warm humidity engulf them, the air conditioning a welcome relief as they walked through the revolving glass door into the lobby.

A smiling staff member welcomed them as they approached the sleek reception area and identified themselves. 'Mr Durante, Ms Morrison. I will have someone take you up to your suite.'

Stella paused, as he frowned. 'A suite?' he queried. 'I requested an additional room for Ms Morrison.'

'Yes, unfortunately the staff member you spoke with made an error. You were emailed back straight after to explain that as we have a delegation here it was impossible to accommodate your request so we simply swapped you to a larger suite at no extra cost. It has two double bedrooms completely separated by a large living area. I know you have business meetings starting from today so I hope this will be acceptable. If not, of course I can try and find you alternate accommodations.'

Max turned to Stella. 'What would you like to do?'

Common sense told him a suite was no different than having adjoining rooms on the same floor. It just *felt* different. More intimate, more personal. But this was personal and they were here to talk in private—a suite might make that easier.

'The suite is fine,' she said, though he saw the small clench of her hands and suspected she shared his reservations.

They followed a bellboy to the suite where Stella couldn't hold back a small gasp. The living area was massive, the polished teak floor dotted with lush sofas and chairs. A state-of-the-art entertainment system and screen adorned one wall, the others were bedecked with a montage of pictures that showed Mumbai through the ages. There was a designated workspace with a sleek slate-grey ergonomic desk and the two open doors showed immense bedrooms.

'They weren't kidding when they said they'd upgraded us.'

'And it's massive, so it *really* doesn't matter that it's a suite,' she said, and instantly bit her lip in clear vexation, and he couldn't help the small rueful smile that tipped his lips.

'So you're saying it *would* be a problem if it was smaller?' he asked.

'Of course not. I just meant...well I wouldn't want to invade your space.' There was a silence that she hurried to fill. 'If you're working or you want to have a meeting up here or...you know what I mean.'

'I know exactly what you mean. Space invasion won't be a problem. But right now you can have the whole suite to yourself. I've got a couple of meetings downstairs. Once I'm back I'll grab some sleep and a shower, then we can head for dinner if you like? Maybe book at the restaurant?'

'Sounds perfect.'

Perfect. Only everything wasn't perfect Max reflected as he rode the elevator down to the ground floor, glanced at his watch to be sure he was on time. Yesterday his life had been if not perfect at least on track, a business marriage in the offing, a trip to India that would combine business and a personal quest for his mother and an exploration of his possible roots. Today he was about to become a father with a woman he hardly knew and yet was attracted to with an intensity he'd never experienced before, one that he could neither fathom or countenance. An attraction that had somehow distracted him from the focus here. That Stella was carrying his baby and she had the potential to take his baby away from him.

But right now he needed to focus on the meeting ahead—with the private detective set with the somewhat daunting task of finding the woman who might be his mother. He entered the meeting lounge, saw the man waiting for him, approached the table, shook hands and sat.

'As you are here we thought we should meet to give you a progress report. And we are progressing, but it is not easy. The woman we seek, Rupali Patel—there are many with the same name as her—we are tracking via social media and other means. We have eliminated many who we know are not your mother. You must understand too that it is possible the woman we seek is not in actual fact your mother, or if she is she will not be willing to admit it.'

'I understand—keep going and keep me posted. Send across the report showing me exactly who is left on the short list.'

'We will. Is there anything else we can help with?'

'N—' He bit the denial off as an idea slipped into his head. A way to find out more about Stella. His instinct told him that Stella was on the level, but legal facts also dictated that she was the one with the power. She had said it herself that she may have decided not to tell him about the baby at all, could marry her aristocrat, could do whatever she thought was best for the baby. So maybe it made sense to find out more about her, set his own mind at rest, make it easier for them to find a path to a good way to co-parent.

Parent… He was going to become a parent. Emotion threatened to flood him, a hapless sense of being out of control and the need to do something, anything projected the idea into a decision.

'I'd like you to do a background check for me on the Honourable Stella Morrison. Utterly confidential. Just an overview to see what she's like.' A qualm struck him and he shrugged it off before his next meeting.

CHAPTER SIX

STELLA HEARD THE click of the bedroom door and turned from the window of the lounge. She gulped, wished that the mere sight of Max didn't turn her into a hormonal mess. But as he stood there, dark hair spiked and shower damp, his shirt top button undone showing a tantalising triangle of flesh, sleeves rolled up to expose forearms that clenched her tummy with desire, her hormones went into overdrive, waved pompoms and set up a chant. Gritting her teeth, she forced herself to smile a calm, poised, civil smile, but then she saw the awareness in his brown eyes, the glint of appreciation and she couldn't help it. Her own smile changed into one of appreciation too, her gaze lingering a fraction too long on his lips.

'How were the meetings?' she managed.

'Good. One was with a Bollywood producer who has asked us on a tour of a film set if you're interested? Followed by a visit to some botanical gardens, where one of their new films is going to stage a lot of scenes.'

'I'd love that.' She really would and now at least she could change the conversation to something practical, could fend off the threatening shimmer of attraction. 'So you're planning on streaming Bollywood movies?'

'Initially, but with the view to a potential buyout or at least a stakeholding in the production company. I prefer that—it gives me more control but it also means I am more involved and invested so the relationship is more likely to thrive. But that does also mean we all have to genuinely get on, or at least all have the same general business outlook. So it's early days. This company was set up five years ago by a superstar couple, Bollywood royalty. Pria and Rahesh Khatri. It gave them control over the films they star in so they want to be very sure I am a viable partner. I hope I am.'

'So this deal is really important to you?'

'All deals are important to me, but yes this one is special and I've got a lot on the line. It's a good fit and it will take InScreen another step forward. And the films themselves—they are like nothing I've seen before… I'd like to be part of this world and I'd like it to become part of my business.'

She could hear the passion in his voice, that love for his business, that commitment and also the excitement. 'So despite how successful you already are you still have that ambition…that drive to achieve more.'

'Of course.' The words simple, and she realised that his drive was an intrinsic part of his being. 'I want InScreen to be the best everywhere—I want people to have access to entertainment, to documentaries, to news to whatever it is they want access to and I want my platform to offer it all. And I'll keep working until I achieve exactly that.'

A sudden pang of envy struck her, that he had found his vocation, that he clearly loved what he did. She could hear it in the deep rumble of his voice, the way his dark eyes shone with determination, the movements of his hands. And that enthusiasm gave him an aura of success, of power, of determination… and hell, the shimmer of attraction had somehow slipped through without her noticing.

He shrugged. 'Anyway sorry to bore on. We should head to dinner. Did you book a table?'

'Actually no. I did some research and if you don't mind I thought it might be fun to go and explore, apparently if we go to Marine Drive there are loads of street vendors that sell the most amazing food and we can watch the sunset which is also apparently a must do. If that's OK?' Everything she said was true but the real reason she'd made the decision was she had no wish to replay their last night together. The drinks, the expensive restaurant in the swish hotel, and then... Nope. This way was safer. Outside, plenty of tourists, fresh air and they could walk with a gap between them.

Perhaps he'd figured the same thing because he nodded with a shade too much vehemence. 'Good idea.'

'Then let's go,' she said. 'I think they'll call us a car downstairs.'

Twenty minutes later they alighted on the wide sweeping promenade that curved in a smooth C shape to border the lapping waves of the Arabian Sea. Stella stood and gloried in the cool evening breeze that ruffled her hair and the folds of her long floral sundress.

'I can't quite believe I am in Mumbai—it's definitely not how I saw my day panning out.'

'It does seem a bit surreal.'

She glanced up at him. 'Even more so for you. I'm guessing you're still in shock. I mean when you woke up this morning you had no idea any of this was happening. That I'd turn up, that I'm pregnant, let alone that I'd be here in Mumbai with you.' Her gaze flew to his, as an unwelcome idea entered her head. 'Were you planning on bringing Dora? For the next stage of your marriage plans?' She shook her head. 'I am sorry that you lost that deal.'

'It is as it is. And to answer your question I wasn't bringing Dora with me. We didn't think that we'd be able to pull off the whole lovey-dovey act for two weeks.'

Stella looked at him. 'Surely Mumbai is the perfect place for a lovely-dovey act. I mean look at it. Look at this.' She spread her hand out to encompass the view. 'You've got the beach, the sunset, the sheer sweeping beauty. And soon all the lights will come on and it will be magical.' She broke off, the adjective conjuring up memories she didn't want to dwell on. 'I mean *beautiful*. The perfect romantic setting.'

'Which would have made it even more obvious that we were faking. I already told you

I'm not really a romantic lovey-dovey kind of guy.'

'Yes, but it wouldn't be that difficult to pretend for a few photo shoots. All you'd have to do was hold hands and…'

'I'm not really a hand-holding kind of guy either.'

Now she turned to look at him. 'You've never held hands with a date?'

A small frown creased his forehead as he thought and then he shook his hand. 'Nope. I don't think I have. I mean it's never been a thing.' As they spoke they headed towards the wall that bordered the promenade and sat down, facing the blue of the waves.

'Hmm. 'So, out of interest what is the longest relationship you've ever had?'

'About six months.' He hesitated and then shrugged. 'Well technically. But I was working abroad for a lot of that time so we probably only spent a few nights together.'

'Just nights?' Not that she could exactly judge, their entire relationship had consisted of one night.

'And days,' he said. 'But only a few over the six months. Perhaps *relationship* is the wrong word. I guess they are more like…interludes. Because right now that's all I have time for. My business, my work takes precedence over relationships, so it wouldn't be fair to embark on a serious commitment.'

Her gaze met his. 'A baby is a serious commitment.'

'I know. But a baby is a completely different type of relationship. It is forever. That relationship would take precedence over business, romance doesn't.'

She studied his face, remembered his drive, his ambition, his passion for InScreen. Would he actually be able to prioritise a child, fit them into his schedule? 'So if I were to call you up to say our child needed picking up early from school because she was sick and you were in a business meeting you'd leave to pick her up?'

'Yes.' He frowned. 'Sorry, that was too glib. If she was seriously ill of course I would drop everything and go. If not then it might depend on my schedule. I wouldn't lose a multimillion-dollar deal, and I wouldn't walk out of a meeting if people's jobs or livelihoods were at risk. But I would send someone she knew to get her. I would not let her down.'

'But you would let a date down.'

He shook his head. 'No. I am always upfront with dates that any interlude is exactly that, a temporary period of time devoted to pleasure.' And there it was again; she was sure he hadn't intended it but the words triggered memories of their time together and the sheer intensity of the pleasure.

'I remember,' she said, aware that the words had way too much wistfulness in them. 'I mean you were completely upfront, completely clear what was on offer and that business came first.'

'Until now,' he said.

'Until now. Because now everything has changed.'

They looked out over the sea and she caught her breath as the sun began its descent towards the horizon, the colours tinging the sky with a flood of orange-gold rays and the sky morphed to a purple-indigo backdrop. The whole spectacle filled her with awe and she continued to watch as the colours slowly faded to a deep pink that tiptoed across the dusk. 'It's so beautiful and right now it feels ridiculously symbolic. At the risk of being dramatic it feels like the sun is setting on one phase of my life.'

'In some ways it is. But it's the future that matters.' A future that they were going to share and instinctively as they stood and watched the final fingers of sunshine tiptoe over the darkening blue of the sea, she moved closer to him.

'A future with no regrets?' she asked softly. 'For business deals, for life plans gone awry.'

'There are other deals. There always are.' And she knew he'd go after every one. 'Right now the most important thing to consider is the baby and how to move forward. Without regret.'

'So you have no regrets?' she asked softly. 'About the baby.'

'No, I don't. He or she didn't ask to come into this world. We made this baby—he or she is part of us and I can't regret that.'

'Thank you.' And she meant it; his words were sincere and now she felt sure that he did want the baby. Turning to face him she brushed her lips against his cheek. The sensation so sweet, and yet so sensual and she heard him catch his breath, felt something shift in her chest as she moved backwards, looked at him wide-eyed. God—how she wanted to kiss him again, kiss him properly, tangle her fingers in his hair, press her body against his.

Not happening.

She jumped off the wall, sacrificed grace for speed. 'Why don't we walk for a bit? Look for food.' The words tumbled from her mouth. 'I am really looking forward to this—in fact it's the first time I've felt properly hungry since I've been pregnant. I'm trying to eat right for the baby, but it's difficult when all you want to do is throw up. But right now I am starving.' Excellent, she'd now mentioned throwing up—well at least that should kill the mood.

'Good idea,' he said. 'Let's find food.'

Max took a moment before he slipped off the wall to make sure he had himself in hand; he didn't want to show what effect her proximity, the gentle brush of her lips, had had on him.

He glanced at Stella, silhouetted in the pink rays. She looked stunning, her blonde hair was caught up in a clip and few corn-coloured tendrils framed her exquisite face. The simple flowing dress highlighted her slender silhouette with the faintest hint of a baby bump, and that outline caught his breath with a sense of awe. Her blue eyes met his and he saw her gulp and now his gaze fixed on the slender column of her throat. Dammit—he jumped off the wall to land by her side.

'Let's go.'

Yet as they walked towards the stalls he was suddenly aware of an urge to take her hand, just to see what it felt like. Ridiculous. Unobtrusively he moved a little further away to avoid the chance of their fingers so much as brushing against each other.

'And let's make the most of you being hungry. Anything you feel like eating we'll find it.'

'What if I wanted something home-cooked? Would you be able to do that?'

'Ah. That might be a bit more difficult. If by that you mean cooked by me. No promises there. I mean some days I eat a bowl of cereal for my dinner.' He broke off as she gave a peal of laughter. What?'

'Somehow the idea of Max Durante, millionaire CEO eating a bowl of muesli for his dinner seems…well it's not what most people would imagine.'

'Muesli is when I'm eating in style,' he admitted. 'Mostly it's cornflakes.'

'So what else do you eat if you're home alone?'

'Cheese on toast is a speciality and I do

have a signature pasta dish, spaghetti *al olio*. But I'm afraid that is my repertoire. Quick and easy food—I mean food is just food.'

She shook her head vigorously, genuine horror on her face. 'How can you say that. Food is…food is one of the most important things in the world.' He recalled the way she'd selected from the menu in Dubai and knew she meant every word.

'Well yes—obviously it's important to eat but…'

Another shake of her head. 'No no no! Food is something joyous. I love trying new food, new recipes, and most of all I love eating it. I mean you eat three meals a day every day—surely it's a chance to make sure you're definitely happy three times a day. It doesn't need to be gourmet food, but you can make sure your cheese on toast is special—you can add chilies, or coriander or marmite.'

'Or I'll stick to trusty cornflakes.'

She sighed theatrically. 'Well at least come and give some street food a try.'

They headed towards the line of street vendors who had congregated and he watched as she studied each menu—couldn't help but smile at the look of focus on her face, the intensity of her frown, the way she tipped her head to one side as she studied the choices.

'You do take this seriously.'

'Absolutely. It's important to make the right choice. There is *nothing* worse than choosing the wrong thing and then regretting it.'

'*Nothing* worse?'

'Right now, yes. So I think I'm going to have the *vada pav* and then come back for the *bhel puri.*'

'Why don't you choose for me and then if you don't like what you've chosen we can swap. Because I'll be fine with anything and if I don't love it I'm not fussed.'

'I've got a better idea. Let's both have the same things.'

'Why is that a better idea?'

'Humour me,' she said and as she should stood there, a speculative look in her blue eyes and a smile on her lips, his breath caught in his chest. Again.

And he tried a theatrical sigh of his own and felt an out of proportion happiness when she chuckled. 'I have the feeling I'm going to regret it but OK.'

Once they'd bought the food they wandered back to the wall and perched on it facing each other, the sea breeze ruffling her hair. 'Right,' she said. 'You go first. I want you to close your eyes when you have your first bite. And really, really savour it. Don't think about it as just food, think about it as texture and flavours and spices and then I want you to tell me about it. What it tastes like. See if you can identify the spices.'

'Do I have to close my eyes?'

'Yes. You said you'd humour me and now you have to. It'll make you think about what you eat and make you enjoy it more.' She looked at him. 'Surely intensifying a sensory experience can only make it more pleasurable? A wise man said to me once a long time ago that a lifetime without a spark, sounds… flat, dull, boring.'

'I wasn't talking about food.'

'I know. But to me a lifetime without really tasting and savouring and appreciating food sounds flat, dull and boring.'

'OK… OK. I'll give it a go, but I'm not sure I even know any spices.' He closed his eyes and took a bite of the potato patty encased in a white roll and to his surprise it did feel different to be eating and concentrating solely on the experience of eating.

Focused, chewed, swallowed and opened

his eyes to see her watching him expectantly. 'OK. Go ahead.'

'The potatoes are the perfect texture, soft and fluffy but not soggy, and the coating they are cooked in is perfect, so there is still a bit of texture to each bite and that contrasts well with the fluffiness of the roll. As for the spices as I said I don't know what they all are but I am pretty sure one is fresh coriander and I can taste a hint of heat and there is definitely some garlic and that's as much as I can say.'

'See, that wasn't so hard?' Her smile was wide and as he smiled back the whole promenade lit up as the massive crescent-shaped sweep of coastline illuminated with miles of sparkling lights. 'Look. They call it the Queen's Necklace because it looks like a pearl necklace,' she said.

'It's beautiful.' But really he meant that she was beautiful. 'Now it's your turn.'

'I…' She tucked a tendril of hair behind her ear and looked down at the *food in her hand*, then back at him and now her gaze rested fleetingly on his lips, before she closed her eyes and bit into the *vada pav*. Once she'd eaten she opened her eyes and considered. 'I can taste coriander but also a hint of cumin and maybe the sweetness of cardamom and a tang of saltiness.' Now her gaze rested on his mouth and her voice was low, almost husky and whilst he told himself she was taking about the patty it didn't feel like that. It felt like she was talking about a kiss, about how it had felt to kiss him, how it would feel if they kissed now.

He took another bite and now their gazes were locked. 'I am savouring the heat of the spice and the warmth of the filling and that feeling of newness and unfamiliarity of taste. And that makes me want more, want another bite and another taste, to immerse myself in the experience. The heat, the taste, the spice, the crave for more.'

Her eyes darkened and now he knew that it was impossible to change the momentum—impossible for his brain to override the inevitability and that realisation was as close as he came to even trying. Instead he leant forward and she was close, so tantalisingly close when the swoop and dive of a seagull broke the moment, flew so near he could see the detail of its beak, felt the tip of its wings nearly brush his cheek.

Stella gave a small cry as she moved backwards and he instinctively turned to shoo off the bird and make sure she was protected.

Once the bird was gone he turned, saw that she had retrieved the food. 'Are you OK?'

'Yes.' She rose to her feet and he could see from her closed expression, the look that he'd come to think of as her stage presence, that she had no intention of discussing the near kiss. And that was fine with him. 'And I've got an idea what we should do now. Let's go back to the hotel and I'd like to watch a Bollywood film. Before our tour tomorrow. We can take the rest of the food back.' Her voice was a tad brittle, a little too high-pitched and he hesitated, wondered if they should talk about it. But what was the point? They both knew the attraction existed and they clearly both knew it was a bad idea. Perhaps the distraction of a film was exactly what they needed.

He nodded. 'We could watch one produced by the company I'm in talks with starring the celebrity couple. I've watched a few but not all.' He glanced at her. 'We could order popcorn as well?'

'Sure.' And put the bowl between them as a barrier. This would be fine.

CHAPTER SEVEN

HALF AN HOUR later they were back at the hotel, TV set up and the popcorn in place as planned. Max wondered if he should even sit on the same sofa but in the end it would be even more awkward if he didn't. So the popcorn plan would have to do. He closed his eyes—how had he come to this? Relying on some popped kernels covered in salt to save him from attraction. Self-control much Durante?

He sat down, saw that she too was sitting in a way that indicated a high level of tension, back ramrod straight, knees pressed together, legs turned at an angle away from him. A mirror image of his own body language.

'Right. Let's press Play,' he said in a voice that boomed false joviality.

And then the movie started and slowly, imperceptibly he was drawn in, the magnificent grandeur of the sets, the sheer colour, vibrancy and over-the-top extravagance of the costumes, the authenticity and detail of the props and above all the emotion, the twists and turns of the love story, the betrayals and the passion and the sheer drama so beautifully portrayed.

And somehow as all this had unfolded, and he truly had no idea how, the bowl of popcorn had been moved to the floor still half-full, Stella was curled up with her legs tucked in beneath her, right up next to him, her head on his shoulder one hand tightly gripped in his.

He blinked, remaining still, not wanting to break the moment, the tickle of her hair against his cheek, the sound of the music as the credits rolled, half of him still immersed in the world portrayed by the film.

Stella sat up, wiped her eyes. 'That was amazing.'

He could smell her shampoo, a clean floral-tinged smell that brought memories cascading back, triggered by her proximity, the way she fit in next to him, waking up next to that same scent, the tickle of hair across his chest, her head resting there, her body encased in his arms.

As he looked at her he saw a fresh teardrop sparkle at the end of her lashes and he couldn't help himself. Oh, so, gently he reached out and caught the drop on the tip of his finger.

Heard her shuddered intake of breath and now pure instinct took over, and he leant forward; and there was Stella, her blue eyes wide and full of wonder and want and then they were kissing and it was everything he'd expected and more. The taste of spices, the tang of salt from the popcorn, it was all so right, so welcome, so glorious and as he deepened the kiss her gasp of pleasure, the feel of her fingers in his hair, surged desire through him. Time suspended into a moment of pure pleasure, every sense heightened to perfect pitch until inevitably reality intruded, as the film credits ended and an ad blared from the screen.

Stella pulled away with a small gasp that he recognised as one of distress and he saw dismay transcend desire on her face. Dismay and self-recrimination.

'Dammit!' Her fists clenched, nails digging into the palm of her hand. 'What is wrong with me?'

'Nothing,' he said. 'Or if there is, the same thing is wrong with me.'

'We shouldn't have done that.' Now she twisted her hands together on her lap.

'No,' he agreed. 'But we did.' He reached out and took her hands, gently disentangled them and smoothed away the marks from her nails and even now there was still the jolt of desire, but he ignored it, refused to so much as acknowledge it. 'Stella. It's OK. We shouldn't have done it, but there is no harm done. It was one kiss. We have a massive amount of chemistry and we're spending a lot of time together and…it happened.' He frowned at her expression, could see that his words were having no impact. 'But you are clearly upset—so you do think harm has been done.'

She looked down at their clasped hands. 'Not exactly, but I do know we need to sort this out. Figure out how to not have chemistry, or at least get it under control. The most important thing now is the baby. I need to be focused on working out the best way forward for him or her and I don't want my judgement to be affected by this.'

Fear inserted an insidious tendril at her repeated emphasis on the fact that she was the one making the decisions. Fear and affront that she believed she needed to figure it out on her own, and that meant she still didn't see them as a parenting unit.

Dropping her hands he tried to keep anger and hurt from his voice. 'So you're worried that I may be a bad bet as a father but you won't notice because of our chemistry.'

'No. Or not exactly. I mean *we* are here to try to work out what to do next and I can't work out a strategy when attraction is in the mix. It's messing with my head and I am worried it is making us both see each other through rose-coloured spectacles.' She tried a smile. 'Or if not rose-coloured, whatever the colour of desire is.'

Dammit. Stella was right. Distracted by desire, by this burning need to reach out, to touch, to kiss, to run his fingers through her hair he'd taken his eyes off why they were really here. His agenda. To make sure he was part of the baby's life.

'You're right. We're here to work out a parenting plan and we need to be focused on that. On getting to know each other as future co-parents.'

'Yes.' But he saw sadness touch her eyes. 'That's it. And that is how it will always be so we have to knock the attraction on the head now. Because if we don't, what happens?'

It was the wrong question. Because it was all too easy to imagine exactly what would happen if they succumbed—to picture her in his arms, in his bed. But then what?

'Where would it end?' she continued softly. 'We can't be an interlude…together for a few nights and then go our separate ways. We're in this together forever and I don't want our child to grow up feeling embarrassed because he or she can sense something between us, or even worse that he or she grows up hoping we'll get together. It would all be too messy and complicated.'

'I get it.' And he did. He hesitated, saw that anxiety still etched on her features. He moved closer. 'But please don't feel like we've done anything wrong. We haven't. This…whatever it is between us…this chemistry…it's what created our baby. No regrets, remember?'

She placed a hand over her midriff and now she smiled, a slow, serene smile. 'No regrets,' she said.

'And no harm done. It's good we've had this talk and we can move forward. I know the attraction won't just disappear, but as long as we don't act on it, it will fade away in time.' Though for some reason the idea felt bleak, that something so vibrant, so vital, would slowly dissipate, crumble from rose to ash. But then his gaze fell to her hand and he knew that it didn't matter. Nothing mattered except the baby.

From now on in he wouldn't forget that; this past day had been hazed by attraction. No more. From now on it would be all about the baby, all about making sure he was there for her.

CHAPTER EIGHT

THE FOLLOWING MORNING Stella studied her reflection in the mirror and gave a small nod of approval. A linen jump suit, hair pulled back in a ponytail, flat black sandals, light layer of make-up. Today heralded the return of poised, cool, together Stella ready to assess Max without the rose-coloured spectacles of desire. Because that was what she was in Mumbai for. To figure out whether Max would be a good dad and how much involvement he wanted. No, she corrected herself, not how much he wanted, how much he should have. After all her own father had *wanted* to run her life, *wanted* to make Adriana's a misery, had wanted control.

Determination bolstered her as she entered the living room, a civil, aloof smile firmly in place. And if it faltered slightly, if desire twisted through her at the sight of his sculpted, sun-kissed, muscular arm high-lighted by the bright white T-shirt, the clean lines of his face, the strength of his jaw, the firm line of his mouth—well that was be-tween her and her hormones.

Her own thoughts seemed mirrored in his brown eyes and she could see that he too was different today, sensed that he too had de-cided to adopt a different approach; it was in the stark white of his shirt, the sharp crease in his trousers, the way he held his body, as though he were ready for anything.

'Good morning.'

'Good morning. I've ordered room service. I've got a meeting at eleven but until then we can talk.'

'It sounds like you have an agenda.'

'Nothing so formal,' he said. 'But I would like to know more about you, seeing as you are the mother of my child and I'm sure you have questions too.'

She knew that this was the right way for-ward, knew that it was what they had agreed to, but dammit she missed the ease, the ban-ter…she missed the rose-coloured spectacles. Missed the laid-back Max too. This was the Max Durante who had built a business up from nothing.

A knock on the door heralded breakfast and she smiled as the hotel staff pushed the trolley forward, covered in dishes topped by silver domes. 'We have masala *dosas* filled with spiced potatoes and a Maharashtrian speciality, *sabudana vaad*, which are sago fritters served with our chef's special yoghurt sauce.' The waiter nodded towards Max. 'As you requested all the ingredients are listed out and no unpasteurised milk has been used.' He indicated the other covered dishes. 'Under these are fruit and yoghurts and pastries.'

'Thank you. We can take it from here.'

'It all looks amazing,' Stella added, waited for the waiter to leave and then smiled at Max. 'Thank you for this and for checking the ingredients.'

'I know unpasteurised milk isn't OK, but I wasn't sure if there was anything else.'

'This all looks fine. Better than fine.' Warmth touched her that he had found time to research and had then done something about it.

'Help yourself.'

She heaped her plate and then tasted the *dosa* closed her eyes to savour the crisp lightness of the rice pancake and the contrasting spicy tang of the potato. 'This is to die for. What do you think?'

'It's good,' he agreed. 'Really good. I was reading up on it and the baby is probably able to taste some of the flavour of what you are eating—which is fascinating. Nerves from taste buds begin connecting to the brain at about thirteen to fifteen weeks.'

'I think I am going to try to introduce as many flavours as I can and then maybe the baby won't be a fussy eater.'

'Or maybe he or she will grow up to be a world-famous chef.'

'Perhaps we should just refer to the baby as 'she' from now on.' That felt better to her, a reminder that she really didn't mind the baby's gender, that she was nothing like her father, didn't crave a son and heir.

'That's fine with me.'

'And maybe she could just be a good cook, or someone who loves food,' Stella said softly. 'I don't ever want her to feel pressured to do anything,' she added fiercely. 'I want her to choose a career and I will support that choice and if she doesn't want a career but wants to go travel the world or...volunteer or...well whatever she wants to do I'll help her do it.'

Would never steer her child towards a destiny that she had mapped out for her.

Max nodded. 'Of course, but it will be important to encourage our child too, introduce them to lots of options and whatever she chooses, she should be the best they can.'

Stella frowned... 'As long as she gets to choose.' What if Max wanted his child to inherit InScreen, brought them up to believe that was their path?

'Which brings me to something I'd like to know. What did you choose to do? Your job?' He poured more coffee as Stella looked at him, suddenly loath to answer the question as she remembered the extent of his success, the grit and determination and drive he possessed. He waited a polite second and continued. 'Also what are you planning to do about work? When the baby is born.'

A sense of panic was beginning to unfold, a fear that he would ask all these questions and find her wanting. Because she didn't have any answers. She fought the instinct to put her cutlery down and fold her arms. She was the Honourable Stella Morrison, beautiful, sought after, social goddess and countess material, the woman who had been going to save her family home. True her entire raison d'être had been summarily removed, she was pretty much homeless and jobless, she'd precipitated her father's heart attack and let her sister and mother down *again*, but she was damned if she'd show any vulnerability to Max. Because she couldn't afford to. Because somehow now that the rose-coloured spectacles were off, she was feeling judged.

'Is that the most important thing to you? My job?' The question a prevarication, to buy time.

'No, it isn't. But I am interested and I do want to know how you are planning to juggle work and a baby and how I can help with that. I wasn't aware your work was a state secret. Perhaps you are a spy?' He sipped his coffee and raised his eyebrows. 'But either way I get the feeling you're avoiding the question?'

'I'm not.' She found herself touching the tip of her nose, almost as if to see if it had grown Pinocchio-style. 'I just don't think it will tell you anything deep and meaningful. My job history is more a question of doing 'this and that.'

'Define *this and that*.'

'I've worked as an interior designer and an events manager and I worked in retail for a while as well. But in the last couple of years I was…well practising to be a countess.' She picked up a fritter, took a bite, focused on the crunch of peanuts and chillies and the cooling sensation of the yoghurt. Told herself not to sound defensive. 'As you know I intended to marry into high society to save Salvington and I wanted to be sure I was good at what I was doing. That I could deliver. So I accepted an allowance from my parents and I organised events, I hosted dinners, I learnt how to run a big house as economically as possible, I sat on charitable committees.' The last had in fact been what she had enjoyed most; and what she'd enjoyed most hadn't been the glitz and glam of the events themselves but the behind-the-scenes involvement, the personal anonymous work she undertook that not even her sister knew about.

'So if you had to do your duty and be countess then you were going to make sure that you were the best countess possible?' he asked.

'Well yes. That made sense to me. I was essentially brokering a marriage deal and I needed to make sure I could deliver what I said I would deliver.'

'Understood.' He hesitated. 'But is that

what you wanted to do? I mean I respect your decision to do it. For your family home. But did you *want* to be a countess? Do you think you would have been happy?'

She considered the question, couldn't see any harm in answering honestly. 'I don't know. I wouldn't have been unhappy. I'd have had a family. I'd have saved my ancestral home.' She'd have finally made things up to her sister and as mother of the heir to Salvington she would have had power over her father. Perhaps finally her mother could have left her marriage without fear. All of that would have made her happy and she realised she hadn't really thought much beyond that. 'But hearing you describe how you feel about your job, how it drives you, how passionate you are about it… I didn't feel like that about being a countess.'

'Is there a job you do feel passionate about? What did you want to be when you were a little girl?'

Stella hesitated. This was something she hadn't spoken about for years, had buried away as something that quite simply wasn't possible. But somehow here and now she wanted Max to know, to understand that she wasn't some entitled frippery, shallow person. Or at least that if she was it was a choice she'd decided to make.

'When I was younger I wanted to be a lawyer.' It had seemed clear to Stella from a young age that life wasn't fair. It wasn't fair that her father treated her with so much love and treated her sister like dirt. It wasn't fair that he blamed his wife for all their misfortunes and so their love had shrivelled into a bitter parody of a happy ever after. It wasn't fair, come to that, that the law said she couldn't inherit Salvington simply because she was a girl. So she'd wanted to become a lawyer, understand the law, help people fight unfairness.

She saw the surprise on his face and her eyes narrowed. 'I'm guessing you thought I'd say fairy princess or something along those lines.' And she could hardly blame him really.

'Perhaps,' he conceded. 'But I accept I was wrong. What happened to that ambition?'

'I realised I had to make a choice.' She'd told her father what she wanted to do and to put it simply he'd vetoed it. Told her it would take too long, that her priority had to be Salvington. And when she'd shown signs of digging her heels in he'd done what he'd always done. Taken out his anger with her on Adriana and his wife. And soon after that he'd embarked on his affair in an attempt to father an heir.

All Stella's fault, another consequence of her actions. And everything had spiralled from there, the scandal, her father's return to the marital fold, her own pathetic rebellion that had nearly triggered another tragedy and after that Stella had accepted her lot, had no intention of precipitating any more misery.

But she could hardly tell Max any of that, wouldn't expose her own folly. She'd worked so hard to try to put it behind her, to shut it away and move on. She'd built a new Stella Morrison, poised, cool, the perfect Lady and that was the person she needed to be and so she shrugged, regretted even mentioning the whole lawyer dream. A pointless dream that had caused misery.

'It fizzled out really. I made the choice to embrace the life that I was destined for. And what wasn't there to like about it? I had money, an amazing social life, I enjoyed the jobs I did and it was the right thing to do. For me. Being a lawyer wasn't.' She could hear the hint of defiance tinged with defensiveness in her voice, saw a small frown crease his forehead as he studied her expression. 'I guess I am more the princess type. Easier. More fun and it meant I could save Salvington.'

He looked as though he were going to pursue the subject, but to her relief instead he shrugged. 'Fair enough. But where does that leave you now? Jobwise.' The frown deepened. 'And where will you be living? At Salvington?'

'No. We have a flat in London.' Though the 'we' was perhaps ambiguous. Technically the flat like everything else belonged to her father, but Stella had always used it whilst staying in London. But now? It wouldn't feel right to stay there even assuming her father didn't have the locks changed. That's why she was currently living in… Please don't let him ask.

'So you're currently living in the flat?'

Great. 'Not at the moment. Because it doesn't feel right to do that when my father is still ill.'

'So where are you living?'

'I… Why does it matter?'

'Are you saying you don't want me to have your address?'

'No. I just don't really have an address

right now. I've been staying with friends and in hotels.' She could see him process the words, and come up with the conclusion that she was technically homeless.

'Then I can help. I'd like to help. You're pregnant with my child—you need a proper roof over your head. I'll rent you somewhere. In London would work and if you aren't working right now that's OK too—we can sort something out.'

'No!' The syllable rang out, lacking any cool or poise and she took a deep breath.

She wouldn't let herself become reliant on Max. In any way. Would not give him any power in her life. Been there, done that. Her whole life she'd danced to her father's tune—now she'd dance to her own. There was that panic again because she didn't know the steps, but she'd figure it out and wouldn't reveal even a hint of vulnerability to Max, couldn't cede any power at all.

She'd watched her mother bow to her husband's wishes because she had no choice; Lord Salvington had money, power and position and he'd used them all as leverage, ensured her mother couldn't leave, was reliant on him. That would not happen to Stella and yet…suddenly as she looked at Max all she could see was a man with money, power and position.

Recalled that once her parents had been in love, her mother had trusted her father, and that trust had led to reliance and misery for them all when their relationship had turned bitter, as her father had changed from a loving husband and father into a man turned sour and miserable by the lack of an heir.

'No?' Max's voice held confusion.

'No,' she repeated, more calmly. 'That really won't be necessary. But thank you. I have it all under control.' And there it was— her nose itched again. But this was only a stretch of the truth because she would have it under control. 'I've already got it sorted. I am going back to work at the interior design place.' Talk about winging it and she was more than aware that she was skirting the edge of the truth. But when she'd left they had really wanted her to stay and had told her she could come back whenever she wanted So... 'On a six-month contract and then I'll return when the baby is older. So you don't need to worry—I can pay my bills. And rent somewhere. If you want to help support the baby then I will put aside any money for his or her future. But that's all I will accept.'

He pushed his plate away and she could see the tension now in his shoulders, the set of his jaw. 'So any money I give you now, you won't use to support our child, to pay the bills. You would prefer to live as a single parent where the father refuses to face up to his responsibilities.'

'No. I told you I will save that money for the child.'

'I can provide for my child's future as well as support them in the present. What if she would like ballet lessons or to join a football club?'

'Then I'll pay for that.'

'How? After London rents and bills and childcare how will you do that? I want my child to have the things that I can afford to give, and I don't understand why you would want to deprive her of those opportunities and chances.'

'My child will not be deprived of anything. At all. This isn't about money—there are hundreds of thousands of children who are perfectly happy without expensive classes and material possessions because they have love and care and nurturing and that is a hundred times more important. Ballet lessons do not lead to happiness.' This she knew. 'So if that's all you're planning to bring to the parenting table then…'

'Then what?' he asked and now his voice was low and she could sense his anger, knew that it was justified. It wasn't Max's fault that she was riding a wave of panic, wasn't his fault that he embodied everything she was most fearful of. But right now she couldn't stop herself, braced herself for his anger to escalate and started to utter the words, 'Then maybe there…' is no place for you at the table.

But before she could finish he took a deep breath. 'Stop. Look. I'm not sure what is going on here but maybe we should take a step back. It seems silly to argue about ballet lessons when the baby isn't even born yet, let alone pirouetting. So before you say what you were about to say maybe we both need some space. I'll go down for my meeting and we'll regroup later.'

Surprise held her still for a moment and then she nodded. 'Agreed.'

'But for the record I am not planning to only bring money to the table. I want to be there for my child. 'I want to be part of my child's life, properly, not just a token presence.'

Fear began to circulate—Max would provide pots of money, their child would be caught up in his wealth and fame and glamourous lifestyle, studded with awards and red carpets and celebrities. What if their child preferred Max. Stop. Love was what mattered, not possessions. Really? Possessions had been a balm to her soul in her childhood.

He rose to his feet and she managed a smile of sorts, knew she needed time. To process what he'd said. But also time to call Leila and turn her half lie into a truth—she had to secure a job, had to have her own money, provide her own stability.

Stella waited until he had gone and picked her phone up.

'Leila. It's Stella. Sorry I know it's early.'

'No problem. I'm up and getting ready for work. How are you?'

'It's complicated. But I was wondering if there is any chance I could have my job back. But there is something completely confidential I need to tell you first.'

Quickly she filled her friend in on events without revealing Max's identity. Leila listened and then Stella could visualise her nodding briskly as she spoke. 'Of course you can—in fact by luck my assistant is about to go on maternity leave so I need cover. But it's good you called because I've been meaning to call you. Something odd happened. But this explains it. Someone called me asking for a reference for you? I assumed you must be applying for jobs.'

Stella frowned. 'Nope. I wasn't.'

'Then it's extrastrange because I bumped into Matteo at an exhibition and he said someone had been asking about you. Kind of casually, but he still thought it was a bit off. I put it down to Matteo being Matteo but...'

'But maybe it was a reporter sniffing around.' Stella bit back a groan—the last thing she wanted was for the pregnancy story to break right now, before she and Max had figured out how to handle it. Didn't want her father to be upset, for it to affect Adriana and Rob.

'Thanks, Leila, and thank you for the contract as well.' It would at least tide her over whilst she figured out what to do next. But now maybe she'd do a quick call around and see if she could work out if there was a reporter on her case, though surely they would have tried to contact her direct?

CHAPTER NINE

MAX HEADED BACK to the suite, his mind still buzzing with the results of his meetings, satisfied that they'd gone well, alongside a knowledge that there were still significant steps to be taken to build the right rapport and trust. Just like with Stella.

He sensed he'd somehow overstepped the mark, spooked her, but he'd panicked. Needed her to see, perhaps needed himself to see that he had more to offer than money.

He opened the door to the suite to see Stella pacing the floor. 'What's wrong? What's happened? Is the baby OK?' He strode forward.

'The baby is fine. But I think we have a problem. I've spoken with some friends including my ex—well my current boss—and there has been someone snooping round. I assume it's a reporter, but oddly whoever it is hasn't approached me or my family? But someone is asking questions—and I really don't want anyone to approach my parents for a reaction or for them to see a headline hit or…'

Ah. The penny dropped around about the word *snooped* and Max hurriedly scrolled through his emails, scanned the latest from the detective agency. Yup… 'A detective has undertaken discreet enquiries…'

Max was aware of a craven desire to say nothing, one he dismissed instantly. 'It's not a reporter.'

She came to a stop. 'It's not? How do you know?'

'Because I asked a private investigator to check you out, do a background check on you.'

There was a moment of silence and he watched her expression morph from worry to confusion to understanding and to outrage. 'I— You…*what?* You set a detective on me?'

'Yes. You're carrying my baby and I know nothing about you.'

'I thought that was the point of this time in Mumbai—to find out about more about each other whilst we planned a future for our child and instead you did this. Well, you can forget it, because you are going to have nothing to do with this baby at all.' He could hear anger in her voice, fury, but he could also hear hurt. 'I cannot believe you did something so low.' She shook her head. 'I'm done. I'm out of here.' Grabbing her handbag, she headed for the door.

For an instant Max stood stock still, and then two swift strides took him to the door to look out over an empty corridor. Dammit. He ran to the stairs as he heard the ping of the lift and raced down the stairs, dodged the convention of business delegates with a muttered apology even as he cursed the delay.

Reached the cool marble environs of the lobby in time to see a glimpse of her blonde head as she headed out of the door, raced after her even as his skin went clammy at the instant hit of humid heat.

'Stella.'

She didn't so much as pause as she stormed onto the thronged street, her walk brisk though he was pretty sure she had no destination in mind. Now he didn't even bother with apologies as he thrust his way through the crowds after her, overtook her and turned so they were facing each other, didn't give her a chance to protest before he spoke.

'Because I was scared,' he said. 'That's the answer to the question, why did I do it, why did I have a check done on you?'

'Scared of what? That I'll be a lousy mum.' Hands on hips, eyes ablaze with anger, equally oblivious to the people around them.

'No.' Her words poleaxed him as he saw that her anger masked fear and also disbelief.

She shook her head. 'Why else would you do it, Max? I thought this trip to Mumbai was about us working out what was best for the baby together, a way to make this work. Time to get to know each other better. Not for you to set a detective to questioning my colleagues and my friends behind my back. Whilst plotting to take my child away.'

'I was not plotting to take your child away. At all.' How had he lost track of this conversation so dramatically? 'I was…trying to get to know you better.' Even he could hear the utter inadequacy of the defence.

'I do not need to listen to this. I thought… Oh, it doesn't matter.'

With that she'd dodged past him in a blur of grace and rage and he spun round and strode after her, all too aware how easy it would be for her to be swallowed up by the crowds.

He kept his gaze focused on the bob of her blonde head as she headed towards a massive building, one that rose in a splendour that caught the eye due to it's clearly European architectural style. Stella's stride didn't falter as she plunged into the interior and he hurried after her, instantly aware that the building housed a sprawling market, the interior lit by a stunning fifteen-metre skylight.

Noise, colour and smells all assailed him and for a moment he lost Stella. His gaze scanned the mass of people, roved over the incredible range of goods on display. Brightly coloured exotic fruit, watermelons the size of bowling balls, reds, oranges, yellows dazzled his eyes. Spices pervaded the air, stored in massive sacks—coriander mixed with cumin and the heat of chillies seemed embodied in the bright red cascades that hung in bunches. He recalled Stella's voice describing the taste of the patties just as he spotted her.

'Stella!' his voice was swallowed up in the cries of the vendors, the shouted haggling of the buyers and as he plunged towards her the caw of birds added to the cacophony of noise and he realised he was walking past a pet area. Brightly plumed birds chattered and shrieked amidst the bark of dogs and again his voice was drowned.

On past stall after stall, unsure now if they had circled round, all sense of direction lost and then finally he had nearly caught up with her.

'Stop. Stella. Please.' Perhaps she heard the plea in his voice because she slowed down and then turned, stood in front of a stall selling a vast array of vegetables, and he wished, how he wished that they were here to visit the market, to wander round, could imagine Stella looking at the knobbly kohlrabi, the vivid green garlic stalks, the light yellow lemongrass, inhaling the smell of fresh coriander and enjoying herself. Instead he knew he somehow had to get her to listen, needed to explain, to make it crystal-clear he had no intent to take the baby from her. 'Please give me a chance to explain.'

Her blue eyes narrowed, but then she nodded. 'OK. You've got three minutes.'

He'd take it. But, 'Fair enough. But not here. It's too busy, too noisy.'

Stella glanced quickly across at Max, as they exited the market; rage still churned inside along with a healthy dollop of hurt and she wondered why she was even giving him three minutes when he didn't even deserve three seconds. All that time, pretending to be kind, offering help, kissing her for Pete's sake. And all that time he'd been having her investigated, checking if she would be a good mum.

She increased her stride as he checked his phone looking for a destination. 'There's a park about ten minutes away.'

'Fine.'

Once they reached the wide-open green space, he led the way to a bench under the shade of a massive dark-leafed tree and she sank down with an inner sigh of relief, set a timer and placed her phone on the bench beside her.

Turned to face him, arms folded. But to give him his due, he met her gaze dead on. 'I would never try to take the baby away from you.'

'And why should I believe that?'

He opened his mouth, closed it again, looked down at her phone and then stared straight ahead. 'I grew up without a mother—I'd never wish that on anyone.' The words hit her as she realised she hadn't even thought about his background. 'You can choose to believe that or not. But it's the truth.'

It was, and on a gut level she knew that, but she couldn't leave it at that, not with so much at stake. 'Then why did you do it? What were you scared of?'

'Everything. But most of all I was scared you'd decide to keep the baby from me. That you wouldn't put me on the birth certificate, that you'd move to the Outer Hebrides, that you'd decide I can only have visiting rights once a year.'

'But I wouldn't do that.'

'I don't *know* that you wouldn't. We barely know each other and you were very clear that you could "do whatever you decide is best for the baby". Finding out more about you seemed a good place to start. I wanted to make negotiations easier so I told myself the more I knew about you the better. In truth I felt helpless and I wanted to do something. Because I also grew up without a father and I don't want my child to do the same.'

'I...' Stella opened and closed her mouth; had no idea what to say. She did believe the final call was hers to make but...from his viewpoint, the stance of an abandoned baby...even the smallest chance that his baby would suffer the same way he had must have been terrifying. 'I should have been more sensitive. Because I do want to do what's best for the baby, and I do want you to be part of the baby's life. You are the father.'

'Providing I measure up.'

'Yes. But I should have considered how you were feeling, should have made it clearer that I was starting from the premise that I *want* you in the baby's life. And of course I should have taken your background into account.'

'I don't want your pity.'

'I'm not offering you pity.' She could sense the tension in his body, hear it in the rasp of his voice. 'I'm offering you a qualified apology. And an explanation. I have read so many of your interviews and in all of them you sound so together about your start in life, so understanding of your mother. And because family took you in I suppose I have always read it as a feel-good story, but it's not a story. It's your truth, your life.' And she of all people should know that what you read in the press was seldom the truth. How many interviews had she given where she'd said the right thing, not what she felt? 'And I should have been more careful about what I said.' The timer bleeped and she switched it off, knew this conversation had only started.

He shook his head. 'I don't want you to be careful about what you say. I want you to be truthful. Because I need to know where I stand.' His voice was hard now. 'Because I won't fight to take the child away from you, but I will fight for my rights to be in her life. I have to.'

She could see the shadows in his eyes, the grim rigidity of his mouth set in an uncompromising line and she couldn't help herself, all thoughts of distance gone. Because this wasn't about attraction, this was about the importance of this moment, for them as parents. And so she moved forward, reached out and took his hands in hers. 'I understand and… I don't want to fight.'

She felt some of the tension leave his body, felt a sudden sense of a tenuous connection, a warmth, though there was still a wariness in his eyes.

'And it's not that I have doubts about *you* exactly. But I've been scared too.'

He blinked. 'Scared of what?'

'Scared that you would use your wealth, your position, *your* power to try and take control, to make me do things your way.' Exactly as her father had done. To her, to her mother, to her sister. He had dominated and manipulated, made them dance to his tune and yet he'd claimed to love Stella. And once he'd loved his wife. 'Because that's what happened with my dad. My parents married for love. Once they were happy and if I stretch way back into my memory banks I can remember that happiness. I have a recollection of my father throwing me up in the air, my mother laughing, family hugs. Sometimes I'm not sure if they are real memories or culled from photographs and what my mother has told me. But I do believe once they were happy.'

'And then?' His focus was complete, and she knew he was truly listening.

'Then they weren't. I mean I am sure it's not that simple—their marriage deteriorated, spiralled downwards and somehow that downwards trend wasn't reversible. My father couldn't get over not having an heir. So every month that went past, every year he became more and more bitter over her "failure" and he became more and more cruel.'

Max frowned. 'Then why didn't she leave?'

'My sister and I begged her to, but she wouldn't. Because she was terrified she'd lose custody. My father had everything, the money, the position, the power. He held all the cards and she held none.' She gave a sudden mirthless smile. 'Even when he had an affair and we were hit by scandal, through it all my mother was forced to be the wife who "stood by her man".' She wrapped her arms round her stomach. 'So I don't want history to repeat. I don't want to be reliant on you in any way. Especially as you have so much wealth and power.'

'I understand that.' He hesitated and she looked at him.

'It's OK. I sense a "but". Ask whatever you need to ask.'

'I don't understand why you were willing to marry your aristocrat. Weren't you worried about him using his power or position or wealth?'

Stella blinked, realised the question had completely wrong-footed her with its utter validity.

'It's a good question.'

He gave a small smile. 'I know.'

'For one thing I would have had a pre-nup with Rob.' Though they had never had a chance to get down to the real nitty-gritty of the details, which in hindsight had been foolish. 'But it was more than that. I knew Rob. I don't know you.' But in truth it had been more even than that. With Rob she had been confident that there would be no blips in their marriage, no emotions, no rollercoaster; she'd been sure of her power over him. That she, Stella Morrison, beautiful, poised, sophisticated, was so well-qualified to be Rob's wife,

Countess of Darrow, that it hadn't occurred to her that he had any power. She'd felt safe because there was no spark, no overwhelm of attraction, no…no anything really. 'I liked him, respected him and… I felt in control. Around you I don't feel in control.'

'What about liking and respect?' he asked, but his voice held a soupçon of humour and she welcomed that, relieved that he seemed on board with her explanation, that he believed her.

'I'm working on it.' Her riposte was said lightly and he smiled, a proper smile.

'I have an idea. It's hard to work on liking and respect when we both feel so powerless, so scared that the other one is trying to score points. So why don't we sign a basic initial legal agreement, which acknowledges paternity, that I will be on the birth certificate, but also sets out that neither of us will fight for sole custody with no visitation rights. Then we can build on that as we do get to know each other better.'

'That sounds fair.' It really did and she gave an exhalation of sheer relief.

'Good. I'll get my lawyer to draw something up to send to your lawyer.'

She nodded. 'That works.'

'Good. So now how about we have an ice cream to celebrate? And wander round and look at some of the markets.'

'I'd like that.'

'OK. Well, there's a choice between a spice market or a jewellery bazaar.'

'How am I supposed to choose between those?'

He grinned at her. 'Toss a coin?'

The words took her straight back to their night together, she could almost see the glint of the coin against the Dubai skyline.

'Works for me. She reached into her bag and took the coin out, saw him glance at it.

'Is it the same coin?'

'Actually, yes, it is…' She wasn't sure why she'd kept it. A souvenir of a magical night, a feeling that somehow the whole evening had been precipitated by their decision to talk, to share, to confide. A superstitious belief it was a lucky coin. Who knew? 'Heads for spices, tails for jewellery.'

She tossed the coin, waited for it to land and then checked. 'Tails.'

'Gold it is, then.'

'But ice cream first.'

CHAPTER TEN

MAX FELT A disproportionate sense of satisfaction as Stella tasted the double scoop of cardamom ice cream, her face illuminated by a beaming smile. He could sense her relief and knew it mirrored his own. The idea that they had solved something and taken a step towards co-parenting felt...good.

'Good?' he asked.

'Really good. Truly scrumptious.' Realising what she'd said, she repeated the last words in song. 'I love that film.'

'Me too.' And to prove the point he started to sing the first verse. And after a second she joined in, until she broke off with a sudden gurgle of laughter as a couple of people turned to look at them.

'My mum and sister and I watch it every year—I think they do it to humour me, but I don't care—it's a tradition.'

Envy panged at the idea of a family tradition. 'That sounds nice,' he said.

'It is.' She hesitated. 'Maybe when our child is old enough, we can all watch it together? Let my mum and Adriana off the hook. If you'd like.'

'I would like that.' Appreciated too that she was showing him that she was open to real co-parenting, planned to grant him more than minimal visitation rights.

'Good. It's a date.' And there it was again, that smile that lit up her face and brought the lyrics of the song right back.

'When you're smiling,
It's so delicious
So beguiling,
You're the answer to my wishes.'

'Were films a big deal in your family?' she asked.

'No.' His aunt and uncle had no interest in films, though they had religiously watched the various soaps together every evening, but they had told Max they wanted their 'adult time' and so he had spent time in his room, reading books instead.

He stiffened slightly, aware that he'd tensed

and that she'd noticed. *Careful.* He'd never opened up about his childhood, gone along with the implication that it had been a happy one, partly because it was nobody's business, but also because if his mother was reading any interview he didn't want her to know that it hadn't worked out.

'But then one day I went on a school trip to the cinema and it changed my world,' he said, keeping his voice light and forcing his body to relax. Putting himself in interview mode. Spiel at the ready. 'I loved the visuality of them, the way the actors could make me believe in their characters, so that I actually felt I was in their world and I was fascinated by how books could be made into films and how what was in my head could then be portrayed on a screen and how sometimes a film could actually be better or other times make me rage because they'd changed something fundamental. And it wasn't just films—it was the power of documentaries, the way you can learn and the utter fascination of following the life of a particular animal or species. Or learn history from so many different perspectives—' He broke off. 'Anyway, yes I was always fascinated by film though I never thought I'd make a career from it. Until I discovered you could study film, get a degree. After that everything took on a life of its own.'

The words picked up pace, the well-rehearsed story flowed easily now, well-used during the multitude of interviews he did. Nice and easy, making the segue from childhood to college sound seamless.

'It's great that your family supported you even though they weren't interested in film,' she said, and he caught the wistful note in her voice and suddenly the lie by implication felt wrong, stuck in his craw. Because he knew she must be thinking of her own complicated childhood and the father who had dominated it with his vision for her future and for a moment he was almost tempted to tell her the truth. An urge he shut down instantly, continuing relentlessly on with his story.

'I then went to Harvard to study business and then I combined all my knowledge. I worked hard, I saved and I started a production company with a couple of others. Figured that the way to have best control of what we produced was to stream it myself, set up a streaming company and InScreen was born and now it's here to stay.'

Stella tipped her head to one side, took

another bite of ice cream and he sensed she was going to ask something else about family. Braced himself. 'I know your family died tragically young and I just wanted to say I'm sorry, but I hope they at least got a chance to see you on the road to success.'

'Thank you.' The words sounded muted, and discomfort was a bitter taste in his mouth. But his past was buried. In truth his aunt and uncle had refused to acknowledge him even after his success. He had tried, once he was established, had a job; had contacted them, had offered money to reimburse them for the cost of bringing him up. They had refused, said he 'was dead to them'. Oddly despite everything that rejection, that intractable refusal to acknowledge that they may have been wrong, had stung, 'Money and success don't grant goodness,' his aunt had written. 'Please do not contact us again.'

Soon after he had heard they had been in a fatal car accident. And to his own surprise he had felt grief, because whatever they had done they had tried by their own standards and had at least given him a chance, been physically present unlike his parents. But there was sadness too because their deaths also killed any hope they would change their minds about him.

Stella's blue eyes rested on him and he knew it was time to change the subject, knew he didn't want to directly lie to her, but what was the point of rehashing the past; it wouldn't achieve anything except make her pity him and he didn't want that. But he did now want to know more about Stella and what she really wanted from life.

'So that's enough about my career. I've been thinking and now that you aren't going to become a countess would you reconsider the lawyer idea?'

She hesitated as though she was going to call him out on the abrupt change of subject, but instead she looked away as they left the environs of the park, joined the crowds.

'I'm not sure,' she said. 'It was just a childhood dream really.'

'There is nothing wrong with childhood dreams. What made that your particular dream though?'

'I think I always knew life wasn't fair. It never seemed right to me that I couldn't inherit Salvington, because I am a girl. And that still doesn't seem right to me now. So that isn't fair. But unfairness goes a lot deeper than that.' He saw the shadow that crossed her face and wondered if she was thinking of something specific. 'I mean it's not really fair that my father's wealth and position tethered my mother to him. I got it in my head that if she had someone to turn to who understood the law it could help her, help all of us.

'Then as I grew older I realised how much unfairness there is. I told you that I helped my mother with charity events, well I persuaded her to arrange a fundraiser for women who are victims of domestic abuse and...' He saw tears sparkle in her eyes, saw her jaw set in a determined clench of anger. 'Then I realised my own problems were tiny in comparison to theirs, that even my mother's issues paled in comparison to what some women endure. And these women often have children as well and the law...it doesn't do as much as it should. Everything is so underfunded and so many of these women have no help and don't know where to turn. And yet they are so brave and dignified and so grateful. And their children, what they have seen is heartbreaking.'

Max glanced at her. 'It sounds personal, as

though you have met some of these women, as well as raised money.'

She bit her lip in obvious vexation. 'The money we raised is incredibly important. So far it helped expand a refuge, helped pay for an extra staff member and most importantly meant there was another room available.' She pointed. 'Oh, look. Let's head there. It's another market. Anyway I'm sure you don't really want to know this?'

'Yes, I do.' It was like seeing a whole new Stella, a glimpse behind the woman she presented to the world, the polished, sophisticated society girl. 'And I get that the money is important but if you are involved on a more personal level that is admirable too.'

'No. It's not admirable.' Indignation flushed her cheeks and she looked so real, so vital, so involved he caught his breath. 'What I do is *nothing* and I am certainly not doing it for kudos or to make myself feel good.'

'Why do you do it?'

'Because what has happened to those women is wrong and it's tragic and if I can do anything at all to make their lives even a little better, if it's listening to them, or taking them out somewhere where they can feel safe, or take them out to do something frivolous like have their nails done or look after their children for half an hour so they can rest then I will. One woman is so terrified her partner will find her and take her child away she can't sleep, she feels as though she has to watch over Billy every second. Their life is far away from mine—so no, what I do isn't admirable.'

'Do they know who you are at the refuge?'

'Some of them, but I don't tell them—occasionally they recognise me, but I don't publicise my visits. Partly because I think that would be dangerous, could attract the attention of their partners, give them a clue where they are. But also because this is…'

'Personal. Something you truly believe in.' He could hear the passion in her voice, saw it light up the blue of her eyes, understood too that it was, something she kept to herself because it didn't vibe with the persona she had put together to present to the world. That Stella cared, but not with this raw visceral passion.

'Yes, I do.'

'I can see that, hear that. So why on earth did you give up on the dream to be a lawyer. You said it fizzled out, but I just can't see that happening.'

She caught her lip in her teeth in what he

recognised now as a sign of vexation with herself, when she'd dropped her guard.

'I get you wanted to make a grand alliance but surely you could have done both. Studied law and been a countess.'

'It's more complicated than that.' She turned away. 'In the end the countess lifestyle won out. I figured I could still help people without all the hard work...'

'Stop.' He suited the action to the words, pulled her over to one side. 'You don't have to explain, but please don't lie.'

'I'm not...' She faltered under his gaze.

'I don't buy it—that you gave up a dream you are clearly passionate about for a lifestyle of glitz and glam. I don't and won't believe it.'

Her blue eyes met his and to his surprise she gave a small smile. 'Thank you.'

'What for?'

'For not believing it. And you're right.' She hesitated and then took a deep breath. 'I told my father about my dream to be a lawyer; he took that to mean that I would put off marriage, he was worried a career would take over. So he vetoed it. But I wouldn't back down, I told him I could do both. Save Salvington and be a lawyer.

'He disagreed. That's why he had the affair—he wanted to get another woman pregnant. He called it his try-before-I-buy scheme.' Her voice shuddered with distaste, a feeling he shared. 'Then once she was pregnant he waited for the gender scan. When it turned out the baby was another girl he left the woman high and dry. She went public and then tragically soon after she lost the baby. The whole scandal, the whole tragedy of it all would never have happened if it weren't for me and my desire to be a lawyer. I wish I'd never come up with it, never gone to my father with it. All I did was achieve misery for so many people. So I gave up the idea.'

'No.' He reached out and took her hand. 'No,' he repeated. 'None of that misery is on you. Your father made the choices he made. That is on him. His responsibility not yours.'

'My head knows that, but it doesn't work like that. Because if I had judged him correctly I could have avoided inflicting pain on so many people. On my mother, my sister and that poor woman who he lied to and then abandoned. And who knows if she lost the baby because of the stress of the scandal?'

'You can't take all that onto your shoulders.'

'That's easy to say.'

'I know. I do understand.' He did, recognised the weight she carried.

She shook her head, let out a small puff of disbelief and he couldn't blame her. But perhaps he could help, show her he did get it.

He closed his eyes, wondered if he could do it, share his own burden, realised he wanted to. 'My head knows that it was my mother who made the decision to leave me. That decision to abandon me is on her. But it feels like it's on me. My fault. Because for whatever reason my mother took one look at me and she knew she didn't want me.'

'No.' The word torn from her. 'You don't know that. You can't. There could have been a reason, so many reasons.'

'I have tried to tell myself the same. But if that were the case why didn't she leave something? A letter, a note. Even just to say sorry, or that she lo—cared about me.' Even if she couldn't keep him, couldn't she have left him something, anything, even if it had been a lie.

Her blue eyes had tears in them now, tears that she blinked away as if she knew he would interpret them as pity, and a small part of him wished the words undone, hated to show weakness, hated to show he cared, as though it somehow diminished him. Because he knew there was no point in caring—his mother hadn't cared for him; caring for his foster parents had made the pain of losing them worse. And how he'd wished his aunt and uncle had cared for him even a little bit; in the face of all their loathing he'd always hoped they'd change. Pathetic. And it was time to close this out.

'But I have to try and believe that it's not on me. Not my fault. That whatever her reasons, good or bad, they are hers, her responsibility not mine. But that's hard, so I do understand why you're carrying that load, but you mustn't. Because your father is responsible for his own actions. And that's the truth. You need to try and believe that.'

'And if I promise to try will you try to believe the same about your mother?' She reached out and took his hand in hers, clasped her fingers around the palm and held on and to his own surprise warmth touched him, and some of the tension seeped from his shoulders.

'I'll try. And… I'm truly sorry about the whole private investigator—I should never have done it.'

'It's OK. I wish you hadn't but… I understand. But from now on let's also try and be honest with each other.' She smiled at him, and her fingers tightened round his. 'Deal?'

'Deal.'

'Now why don't we go and explore the market.'

'Good plan.'

CHAPTER ELEVEN

AS THEY WANDERED into the narrow alleyway Stella glanced down and realised they were still holding hands, their fingers firmly entwined. She considered letting go, after all hand-holding was emphatically, surely not a good idea. But it seemed like one right now, after all they had shared. They had made a connection—she sensed intuitively that Max never spoke of his real feelings about his mother, that what he had just done was a road untravelled. Yet he had done it. For her. To make her feel better. After she had shared something—no, some *things*, plural—that she too had never shared before. And she wasn't sure what that meant but she knew something had shifted inside her, broken through a barrier, a guard, and dammit right now she wanted to hold his hand. And the very fact he clearly wanted to hold hers sent a further surge of fuzziness through her.

So for now she was going to hold on and enjoy her surroundings.

And hell, what was there not to enjoy?

The market held her spellbound as they wandered along the multitude of stalls, some of them as tiny as one hundred and fifty feet, others large and imposing, that lined the weave and curve of narrow lanes. All of them doing a roaring trade—the glisten and shine of gold, silver and precious stones dazzled her. People everywhere, some haggling customers, other trying to transport goods through congested pathways, herding bullocks along the side, carrying items on their heads to quicken their progress. Every available space taken up.

'It's like walking through a magical Aladdin's cave; but how on earth would you ever be able to buy anything here? How would you choose?'

'It is a bit daunting, but clearly it works. There are over seven thousand shops in the market, and about sixty-five percent of Mumbai's jewellery trade is conducted here. Literally millions all sprawled out. I have no idea how you would locate a specific shop but some of these businesses have been here for hundreds of years.' She blinked, stopped outside a display—chains, bangles, anklets; the gold so bright and shiny it almost hurt her eyes even behind her sunglasses. 'They're beautiful and they define bling. But do you know what I need now?' she said.

'Food and drink,' he replied promptly.

'How did you know?'

'Lucky guess and you're in luck. Apparently this market is also known for its food. We just need to find the bit where the food stalls are.'

His fingers tightened round hers. He took one last look at his phone and tugged her back into the crowds and ten minutes later they arrived at their destination and she gave a small sniff of appreciation as she inhaled the scent of spice, of frying oil.

'OK. You stay here and I will go and get us food,' he said.

As she eyed the throngs of people she nodded her thanks and settled to wait, watched as he disappeared into the crowd. Just when she'd given him up for lost he returned, balancing a selection of containers and cups on a makeshift tray.

'Here you go. I got *bhel puri* because you

missed out last night and this is apparently unique to the bazaar. I talked to the vendor and checked on line and…among other ingredients we have dry puffed rice, onions and tomatoes, chickpeas, coriander, salt, a squeeze of lemon juice and most important something called *chappan* masala, which is made from fifty-six spices ground into a fine powder. He paused for breath as they wedged themselves in position at the roadside. 'I also have something called *kachori*—which is a kind of flat savoury doughnut filled with spiced lentils. And I have mango and apple juice because I thought that was the best thing to hydrate us.'

Stella looked at him and the sheer thoughtfulness, the fact he'd remembered the *bhel puri*, the fact a man who had no real interest in food had checked and memorised the ingredients all combined to conjure up a warmth of happiness.

'Thank you.' She blinked back a sudden tear and he looked at her quizzically.

'If I'd known it would make you cry I'd have chosen the omelette option.'

'I'm not crying. Or if I am it's hormonal— I just need food.'

'Then I'm your man. Let's share it out.'

'*I'm your man…*' And as Stella looked at him, as she tasted the food, she warned herself not to take those words too literally. Max wasn't anyone's man. But…but he would be in her life forever, because they were bound together by the tiny being growing inside her.

'So what now?' she asked once the last fragrant morsel, the final crumb had been consumed.

'Back to the hotel. I for one could do with a shower and then we can make a plan for the evening. I think we should have some fun; celebrate that we're moving forward together. I'm thinking why not let our hair down a bit, enjoy Mumbai's nightlife—maybe find somewhere that does great food and plays some Bollywood music. Get us in the mood for our tour tomorrow?'

'That sounds…' Dreamy, wonderful, amazing, like a date. 'Fun,' she settled for. This was not a date, and it was not dreamy. But dammit it felt like both.

Later that evening Stella glanced through her wardrobe, wondered what to wear. Knew that she should wear something flattering but conservative, something that was not designed to attract or lure or stage an entrance. Her fingers touched the folds of a grey dress, long, flowing, cinched at the waist with a slim light grey belt, with long flowing sleeves and which would be the correct 'co-parent outfit'.

Or she could wear this…now she pulled out her red dress. Also long, but it left her neck and arms bare and the red material was shot through with a shimmer and a shine and the skirt had a strategic slit down the side, the whole thing designed to attract, lure and scream 'Look at me'.

So what to do?

There was a knock at the door and she turned, called, 'Come in' and gulped as Max entered. Dark chinos, dark collarless button-down shirt and a light jacket—smart but not too formal and he looked gorgeous.

'Sorry. I can't quite decide what to wear.'

'Then you know what to do. Toss the coin.'

'Yup. You're right.' Stella suited the action to the word and looked down. The coin had spoken. The red dress it was.

'Give me half an hour and I'm all yours.'

'*I'm all yours…*' The words danced and shimmered across the room and for some reason she didn't care. Somehow the throw of the coin, the outcome made her want to throw caution to the wind.

'I'll be waiting,' he said.

True to her word half an hour later Stella checked her reflection and a doubt, a qualm flickered. She looked…pretty good, exactly how she'd look if this were a date. Her blonde hair fell in waves past her shoulders, her lipstick matched the dress in shimmer, shine and vibrant colour; her pale pink heels added height and…and maybe she should change?

Nope. There was no harm in looking good—after all she was headed out to Mumbai's nightlife. And soon enough she wouldn't even fit into this dress and…and she wanted to see Max's face.

Swivelling she headed to the lounge and had the satisfaction of seeing him literally gobsmacked.

'You like?'

'I like…a lot.' There was a silence. 'So much that my usual eloquence has forsaken me. You look incredible… Mumbai won't know what's hit them.'

'So the coin chose well.'

'The coin definitely knows what it's talking about. It's a keeper.' He plunged his hand into his pocket. 'And speaking of coins I got something for you.'

'For me?'

'Yes. Here.' He handed her a long flat jewellery box and she opened it, her fingers trembling as she lifted out a necklace. With a pendant hanging from it, a golden coin in a circle of gold—bright, shiny, shimmering gold.

'It's beautiful.'

'I got it at the bazaar, before I got the food. I thought…well I thought you'd like it.'

'I do like it. A lot.' She paused. 'And all my poise has deserted me too.' She handed it to him. 'Would you put it on. Because believe it or not it is perfect for this dress. Which proves that coin has magical powers.'

'Just like me,' he said, and his voice was a deep rumble over her skin and as he took the necklace and their fingers touched a shiver of desire rippled through her. One that intensified as she turned and dropped her head, presented the nape of her neck, heard his slight intake of breath. Then the cool of the gold rested on her skin and now his fingers brushed her nape and she nearly mewled as sensations rocketed in her.

'Thank you,' she said, and she didn't even recognise her voice, breathless, husky and so full of yearning. Somehow she pulled herself together, walked over to the mirror and looked at her reflection; the necklace glinted at her, shone bright against the red of her dress and the blonde of her hair. She met his gaze in the mirror. 'I love it.'

'I'm glad. I... It looks beautiful.'

Every instinct told her to swivel round on her pink stilettos, march over to him and kiss him.

But somehow, somehow instead she held her voice steady and said, 'Right let's go.'

And so half an hour later they headed towards the venue side by side. As they stood outside she craned her neck, looking up at the multi-storied building.

'One of the highest hotels in India,' he said. 'If not the highest, I think. But it also houses this place which is apparently the place to be seen.'

'Is that why we're here? To be seen?'

'No. Well maybe a little—it won't harm to say we visited here, especially as Pria recommended it.'

'Pria Khatri who owns the studio you want to buy a stake in?'

'That's the one. She said she'd speak to the management so we could turn up whenever we want.' He grinned. 'Let's hope she remembered or we'll be bounced out.'

Not something she could envisage happening to Max Durante but she liked that he saw it as an option. 'I'm pretty sure between us we'd sweet-talk our way in.'

In any event they were ushered inside and Stella soaked in the ambiance. Huge leather sofas were strewn over the floor, illuminated by the magnificent brilliance of eclectic chandeliers. But what caught the eye and caused her to stop in her tracks was the view, made all the more stunning by the full floor-to-ceiling windows which made the panoramic Mumbai skyline look so close you could step out into the inky blue sky.

And she couldn't help but recall the Dubai night sky, that magical evening that had started with an equally breathtaking view of a different city. Back then they had one night together, but now...now they were a partnership. And in the here and now that felt...good.

He nodded to the dance floor. 'The Bollywood music is later. Do you want to dance now? Or grab a drink first. Or food.'

'Let's dance and then I'll have an appetite for the food.'

He held out a hand and they headed to join the other people on the wooden dance floor. As the DJ wandered down the decades, providing a medley that somehow morphed the years she decided that she needed to, wanted to lose herself in the moment, and perhaps Max did too as they both immersed themselves in the beat of the music, until she knew she needed to call it and she gestured to the tables.

'I needed that,' she said as she sat down, knew she was flushed and breathless. 'It was exhilarating and it was fun and it kind of regulated my emotions a bit.' A shame it hadn't regulated her hormones. But it hadn't and her hormones weren't helped by the way he looked in the dim lights, his six o'clock shadow gave him an added edge, his hair less tamed, his sleeves rolled up to show off his muscular forearms. Her eyes roved the breadth of his chest and shoulders, and she forced herself to focus on the menu instead.

'You can definitely dance,' he said.

'So can you.'

He shook his head. 'Not really. I took lessons. On how to not make a fool of myself on a dance floor.'

'No way...'

'Yup. First time I went dancing at some corporate do the DJ nearly died laughing. I figured that wasn't going to look good for my image so I took lessons. It took a long time to get me to this level.' He leant forward. 'But if you tell anyone I'll deny it.'

'Your secret is safe with me.' She mimed zipping her lips and locking away the key.

She smiled up at the waiter. 'I'll have a lavender lemonade please.'

'A Glenlivet,' Max said.

The drinks arrived within minutes, mixed behind the massive square bar, which was surrounded by spotlighted bar stools and overhung with a shelving unit that held the most varied assortment of spirits imaginable. They clinked glasses. 'To the future,' Stella said.

'The future.' He paused as the music changed and now it was Bollywood songs that surrounded them, mingled with the chatter of people and the sound of laughter. 'I've been thinking about that.'

'Go ahead.'

'I know this is too soon and I know you probably won't say yes.'

To her horror Stella realised her heart was beating a little too fast. 'Yes.'

'I've been thinking about the future. Your

future. And I want you to consider the idea of becoming a lawyer and letting me help.'

She gave a mental eye-roll—what on earth had she been expecting him to say? Whatever it was it wasn't this and she realised she was already shaking her head. 'I haven't given up the idea, but if I go ahead I'll stand on my own two feet.'

They both looked down at her feet and she smiled, 'Though I may change my shoes first.' Hoped the words would take the sting out of her refusal.

'I'm not offering a handout.'

'What would you call it?'

'Part loan, part investment.' He leant forward, pushed his half-empty glass to one side. 'I get you won't just let me fund you and I admire that. But I can't see why you won't let me loan you some money—we can agree on a repayment plan and it will all be drawn up by lawyers. If we fall out on a personal level it will not affect the loan—neither of us will have the power to do that.'

'So that's the loan. I don't get the investment part.'

'What you said, about the difference between giving money to charity and being more actively involved, on a personal level. I liked that.

'OK. So InScreen does donate to charity. I get employees to vote on which charities they want to support and I know the money goes to worthy causes. But… I'd like to do more.'

'I'm still not seeing how this connects to me.'

'I'd like InScreen to hire a lawyer who isn't corporate, who can actually go out there and help people. I'm pretty sure there is plenty of unfairness in the entertainment world and maybe we need someone to help with that. Someone too who can get involved with our charities. So I part fund you and in return you are on call for InScreen for four years. Again we draw it up legally.' He shrugged. 'Look, I'm thinking out loud here but what do you think? I promise we'll tie it up so I cannot wield any personal power.'

'I…' Stella tried to think; she knew he was wrapping this up to make the help acceptable to her, but knew too that it was a fair offer. Win-win. But had her mother once felt like this about her father? But it didn't matter— Max was factoring in the possibility trust would corrode, was protecting her from the possibility. 'I'll think about it but whatever I decide, thank you.'

'I believe you would make a great lawyer and you'd be an asset, not just to InScreen but to all the people you'd help. So give it some serious thought.' He picked up his drink. 'But enough seriousness.'

Stella nodded, but her brain still whirled, part happiness at how seriously he was taking her aspirations, touched by her belief in him and she gave the smallest of sniffs.

'Hey no crying.' He snapped his fingers. 'I know what to do. I'll tell you jokes.'

'Jokes.'

He nodded. 'I've got a whole list of dad jokes. Guaranteed to make you laugh. Here we go. What's brown and sticky?'

'Um…'

'A stick. How do celebrities stay cool?' he paused and held his hands out in a ta-da gesture. 'They have many fans.'

She couldn't help it, she gave a gurgle of laughter. 'They are so bad.'

'Yup and there are plenty more where they came from. So if you want me to stop, no more tears.'

'No more tears,' she agreed.

Then let's order food. I saw masala fries

and tandoori lollipops and wasabi cashews on the menu.'

'Hand it over.' But not even the menu could distract her from the ever-growing fuzzy warmth and she knew she needed to be careful. But surely there couldn't be anything dangerous about being happy, getting on with the man who was the father of her baby?

CHAPTER TWELVE

'YOU OK?'

The following morning as the car sent by the studio pulled away from the hotel, Max turned to look at Stella, amazed at how fresh and pretty she looked, dressed in simple leggings and a tunic top. A far cry from the glamour of the evening before but every bit as beautiful.

'I'm good. Though some muscles I didn't know I had are aching.' Not surprising after the evening of dancing and laughter they had enjoyed. He grinned. 'As for all the jokes...' Now her laughter pealed out.

'Just make sure you don't bring any of those out at this meeting.'

'No, I won't. Not included in my meeting prep.' Preparation that encompassed amassing knowledge on the company and the two people they were about to meet, along with as much information on Bollywood as he could assimilate.

The limo arrived at the studio and they alighted, entered the reception area where they waited a few minutes before Pria and Rahesh Khatri appeared.

Max reminded himself that first impressions were important, felt as always the churn of nerves, the sense of anticipation, the knowledge that the next hour could make or break the deal. A quick sideways glance at Stella showed a woman who knew exactly how to act, how to work a room, and he was reminded of her entrance onto the rooftop bar in Dubai.

'Max. Good to meet you at last.'

'You too and thank you for agreeing to show us round yourselves. This is Stella Morrison, a colleague of mine.'

'It is good to meet you both and we want to show you round personally, want to make sure you have an immersive experience.'

Stella smiled. 'Can I also tell you how blown away I am with Bollywood films? Max introduced me to your films. Well he said that he started by trying to look at them analytically, but bam... Every single one sucked him in. Then we watched one together, *The Final Ending*, and I still find bits of it coming into my head. And what I really cannot get my head round is the dress you wore for the love scene. I am in awe that it weighs thirty kilograms and you danced in it looking as though it were as light as silk.' She paused for breath and laughed. 'OK I'll stop now. I promised I wouldn't gush.'

The beauty of it was that Stella was genuine—and that was clear.

Pria smiled. 'Gush away darling,' she said. 'An actor is like a porous sponge—we have massive egos combined with no self-confidence. So all compliments are manna.' She turned to Max. 'And I hope you also noted that every one of those films turned a healthy profit.'

'I wouldn't be here otherwise. Though as I discussed with your finance director there are some things that we need to go over. If we get to the latter stages of negotiation. But that is for another time. Today is about this, and for me to get an understanding of everything that goes into your movies.'

'Well seeing as you are here,' Rahesh said, 'Perhaps you would like to see one of the sets from *The Final Ending*.'

'One hundred percent yes,' Stella said.

'Rahesh, I read that you have a lot of involvement with the sets,' Max said. 'I was stunned at the amount of time that goes in.'

'Yes. For this one I commissioned and helped make an exact model replica to make sure we got as much historic detail as possible correct and—actually, hold on. I'll get one of the set managers down to meet you. She did a lot of work on this.'

A few minutes later a woman headed towards them and Max turned to be introduced.

'Max, Stella, this is Rupali. Rupali Patel. She...'

Max froze, the words slammed into him and he could feel the colour ebb from his face, even as he desperately tried to click his brain into gear. The detective had told him it was a common name, that there were scores of people called Rupali Patel.

Yet he couldn't seem to help himself, the words of introduction Rahesh were saying blurred into meaningless syllables and his vocal chords acted of their own accord, broke straight in unceremoniously.

'Rupali. That is an interesting name. I wonder have you ever been to England?' It was gauche, it was uncalled for and he sensed rather than saw the two actors exchange glances, sensed Stella's look of concern.

'I am not sure that is relevant,' Rahesh's voice held a note of irritation, caution even. 'We have many good colleges here and as I was saying...'

Again the words vanished, because she hadn't denied it, surely evidence of a sort and he stepped forward, his eyes devouring the woman in front of him. His eyes scoured her face, trying to assess her age.

Another step forward and now his brain was desperately trying to get his attention, tell him to shut up, to register the confusion on the woman's face but another step as more words fell from his lips. 'And do you have fa—? Agh!'

Pain stabbed his foot, and he was aware of Stella standing right next to him, one hand lightly on his arm, as he bit back a gasp of pain, realised she'd jabbed her high-heeled sandal into him as she broke into speech.

'Max told me there were literally thousands of mirrors used. Is that right? And it was here wasn't it that one of the most moving scenes took place when Lakeesha thought she would never see her lover again and… I wept buckets and I'm pretty sure Max had tears in his eyes too.'

Rupali turned to Stella in clear relief and finally Max's brain engaged, focused first on the pain in his foot, a welcome pain, a distraction that had brought the world back into focus. Now he could see that the woman standing in front of him couldn't be his mother; she was way too young, midthirties perhaps. Knew too that there was every chance he'd blown it—despite Stella's sterling efforts he sensed the actors' wariness, knew they had a reputation for being stellar employers who saw their employees as family. At worst he'd come across as wildly, creepily inappropriate, at best as utterly unprofessional.

But for the next hour he did his best, as Rakesh and Pria showed them the numerous costumes, as they watched a scene being filmed, hoped he managed to get across the enormous amount of research he'd put in, tried too to show that he felt a genuine love for the genre, for the sheer extravagance of it all. Through it all he was silently thankful for Stella, who asked proper questions, made their hosts laugh and shimmered with a serenity he could only envy. And in the end before they left he decided some sort of acknowledgement was in order. 'Thank you for this opportunity and I apologise for my lapse of focus earlier.'

'You wouldn't be human if you didn't lose focus occasionally. You have made it more than clear that your interest in our business is genuine and your track record speaks for itself.'

Husband and wife exchanged glances. 'Why don't you and Stella come to a party we are throwing tonight? Nothing massive, about forty staff and a few friends to celebrate winding up a production.'

'We'd love that.'

'Good. We will see you later and enjoy the botanical gardens.' Pria smiled. 'Imagine me dancing across them.'

As they exited the studio Max wondered if it were possible to pretend the whole humiliating incident hadn't happened. Wished he could close down the aftermath of the shock, his nerves still frayed by the intensity of his reaction. As they climbed into the car he considered cancelling the trip, vetoed the idea as no doubt Pria and Rahesh would ask about them later at the party.

To his relief Stella held her peace for the duration of the car journey, fielded most of driver's conversation as Nihal navigated the stream of traffic, seemingly oblivious to the blare of horns as drivers changed lanes without warning.

She remained silent as they entered the gardens, through a pair of wrought iron gates and they both instinctively inhaled deeply and paused to allow the welcome breeze to cool them down and he took some comfort from the rolling hills and the sound of birds.

'These gardens are by the Arabian Sea,' he said. 'Twelve acres of huge green trees, butterflies, cacti and hundreds of different plants.'

'It's beautiful,' she said. 'The perfect place to come after a shock, or to calm anxiety.' She paused. 'What happened back there? I know how important this deal is to you and how much work you've put in. I also know you don't lose your cool or your nerve easily. So what happened?'

All he knew was that he didn't want to explain, wanted to bury the humiliation, bury his loss of cool, loss of nerve.

'And are you OK?'

That was easier.

'I'm fine.' But the words sounded forced, ragged round the edges. 'Thank you for stepping in back there. I really appreciate it.' OK better, he was back in stride. 'Or should I say stepping on it. My foot is still feeling that move. But it worked.'

'Good.' Her voice even. 'But I think that was a temporary fix. It snapped you out of it.'

'And that's all I needed.'

'What happens if you snap back in? Tonight. At the party.'

He wanted to dismiss the idea as utterly preposterous, but he could still feel the sense of helplessness, the clammy sheen on the back of his neck, the sudden conviction that the woman in front of him was his mother. The freeze of his vocal chords, only for them to utter unscripted nonsense. Throwing his business deal into jeopardy.

What if it happened again? If something or someone else triggered a response. Another Rupali, a mention of a plot involving an abandoned child, a woman who he imagined had a look of himself... the possibilities seemed suddenly endless. Each one engendered a sense of panic, a claustrophobia, a wrench of anxiety to his nerves.

OK. Breathe. He would not let this feeling win—would not lose a business deal he had worked so hard for, wanted so much. In which case he'd have to admit the unpalatable, that he might need some help. Need Stella to step in, as she had before. Do something to pull him out of it before he was gripped by the paralysis, the delusion or illusion.

They continued to walk the wide, sweeping pathway, shaded by a dense canopy of trees that loomed up above them towards the blue of the sky, providing a welcome shade from the sun. Trees that had seen decades— centuries even—go by, had looked over so many people strolling or scurrying past, witnessed so many confidences and declarations and everyday chatter.

A breeze reached them, with a tang of salt and they could see benches overlooking the blue of the sea. Instinctively they both headed that way and sat, facing the water, saw the bob of colourful fishing boats undulate on the indigo roll of the waves.

'You're right,' he said. 'I can't risk that happening again.'

'Then let me help. What can I do?'

He pressed his lips together, told himself not to be a fool. He didn't need to share much, but… 'I guess I'll need you to "baby-sit" me.' The very idea ridiculous. 'Make sure I don't fugue into incoherence again.

And to do that I get you'll need to know what happened.' Stella couldn't help without some background so he'd have to suck it up.

'I've always hoped my mother would come forward.' Each word felt an admission of weakness, of need. 'That she would contact social services in London, or contact me direct if she figured out who I am. I have a pretty high profile and in any interview I've always made it clear that if she came forward I would welcome it. But she never did.

'About a year ago we did a documentary on people who traced their birth parents and it hit a chord in me. There was a woman who found her birth mother and not only that she discovered she had siblings and I thought... that I just wanted to know. Not necessarily do anything about it but to know. So I hired a private detective. Anyway, to cut a long story short they think they may have tracked her down, or at least discovered her name. They believe she that she is half Indian, that she moved to Mumbai some years ago and she is called Rupali Patel.'

He realised he was still staring out to sea, focused on the horizon as though his life depended on it.

'No wonder you reacted like that when you

met Rupali earlier.' Her voice soft, no judgement. 'Your mind went into freefall.'

'I have no idea where my mind went. All I know is that my reaction nearly cost me a business deal.'

'I think you should give yourself a break—it was a massive shock.'

'It shouldn't have been. It was one hundred percent clear that she couldn't be my mother—she was way too young for a start.'

'Yes. But you couldn't have known that in that moment. It is such a huge deal deciding to try to find her and to be here in Mumbai where she may be—of course it will mess with your mind. And maybe it is a bigger deal now than it was when you made the decision,' she said gently. 'Because of the baby.'

He glanced at her, a question in his eyes.

'Technically she will be the baby's grandmother,' she said.

The words hit him with a blast, a knowledge he didn't want. What if the baby was a girl and looked like his mother? What if every time he looked at his daughter he was searching for features of the woman who had given birth to him and then abandoned him? In some sort of horrible echo of history, the way his mother had looked at him and seen his father, seen him in his eyes. What if he saw his mother in his daughter, what if he couldn't deal with that?

'Max?'

'My mother has nothing to do with this baby. When she walked away from that cardboard box and left me inside it she walked away from any rights to be a grandmother. So I am going to call the private investigator off. You're right in that she is technically the baby's grandmother, but it's going no further than a technicality.'

Stella's eyes widened. 'That's not what I meant.'

'I know. But it's what I mean. Thank you.' He rose to his feet. 'Shall we keep walking? There are some beautiful viewing points and I promised Pria we'd look at the butterflies.'

As they walked, surrounded by the beauty of the trees and plants Stella glanced at him, her mind racing, as she tried to think what to say, what to do. In truth she was still reeling herself from his reaction to Rupali, tried to imagine how he must have felt in that split second when he believed he was face-to-face with his mother.

His face had drained of colour and the anguish, the pain, the hope in his eyes had torn at her heart even when she hadn't known the origin of his emotions. But now she realised just how deep his abandonment had gone, what wound it had inflicted.

Yet now… now he was going to abandon his search when he was so tantalisingly close, ostensibly for the baby, but she suspected it went deeper than that. That exposing his emotions like that had made him feel vulnerable, weak and that meant he was closing it all down.

'Max?'

'Yes.' His voice even, guarded, remote even, but she gritted her teeth, wanted him to open up to her.

'I know it's not my decision but I don't think you should call off the detectives.'

'I don't want to complicate things.'

She took a deep breath. 'Things are already complicated and this is your opportunity to find answers that you've wanted all your life. You said you made this decision because you wanted to know.'

He shook his head. 'Now I've realised I don't. She did what she did. It doesn't matter why.'

'Doesn't it? If there are extenuating circumstances or at least an explanation for why she did what she did. Perhaps she regrets her decision. Believes it was a mistake.'

Just as she regretted so many decisions in her own life. Deeply regretted the way she'd treated Lawrence.

'Then why not contact me?'

'Because she knows you've had a good, happy life without her so she wants to leave well enough alone.' Again exactly as she had done with Lawrence. 'But that doesn't mean she doesn't have regrets. And it doesn't mean that you don't deserve answers.'

'I'm fine without them, fine without her. I've survived—dammit I've thrived without her.' They kept walking, headed now towards a large wooden viewing structure, a vantage point to watch the butterflies from and her brain swirled with thoughts.

Max *had* made a success of his life, and yet when he'd seen Rupali, believed she was his mother, that mask of success had slipped, showing the rawness of emotion, the vulnerability underneath. And something struck Stella, a deep sense of compassion, of caring for this man. One she refused to question or analyse, but she wanted to help him, wanted him to open up to her, to drop his guard. So perhaps she needed to drop hers.

'You have thrived without her, but that doesn't mean what she did doesn't hurt and maybe you should find her. Get the explanation you deserve, because that might give you closure.' Just like she should have spoken to Lawrence, told him the truth, instead of running scared after the tragic horror of their breakup, a tragedy brought about by Stella's mistakes. And now a different type of guilt touched her, that she had made bad decisions and not had the courage to face up to the consequences.

But she hadn't convinced Max, she knew that, knew that he'd hated the earlier rush of emotion he couldn't control, wouldn't risk a repeat. But if he buried it, walked away, that was wrong too.

They reached the viewing structure and started to climb the winding stairs. With each step Stella tried to decide what to do and once they reached the top they looked down over the massive trees, palm trees and magnificent weeping willows and she could see the colourful flotillas of butterflies circling, delicate flutters of orange and red and purple. And she knew what to do.

She turned to face him. 'You deserve to know what made your mother do what she did—whatever her reasons. I know you do, just like I know she may regret her decision even if she hasn't contacted you.'

His mouth set in a line of scepticism and she couldn't blame him.

'I know because I've made some decisions I regret with all my heart.' She could hear the question in the silence, carried on the beat of the butterflies' wings and she continued to talk.

'After my father had that affair I was consumed with anger. I couldn't believe that he would have abandoned me, shipped me, my sister, my mother out of Salvington, replaced us all. It was a betrayal and I wanted revenge of sorts. So I decided to go off the rails and to find myself a truly unsavoury boyfriend, to help me do that, the sort of person my father would hate. And so I targeted Lawrence. He was perfect, not because I was attracted to him or anything, but because I knew if I hooked up with him my dad would go ballistic. He was everything my father hated—rich, yes, but nouveau riche, and in addition he had piercings, tattoos, tatty torn clothes—as far away from an aristocrat as you can imagine. So I decided to lure him in—I didn't even think about how it might affect Lawrence, all I thought about was me, me, me. That was bad decision number one.'

He didn't say anything but she sensed how intently he was listening.

'Lawrence fell for me, big time. And I couldn't cope—he said he loved me, needed me, wanted me and all I really wanted was to use him, be seen with him, play the role of rebel aristocrat taking the wild path. I wanted to be pictured wine bottle in hand outside the latest cool nightclub and irony of ironies he wanted to stay in and talk about our future. I knew I was in over my head but I kept telling myself it was OK, he couldn't really love me—not when I didn't love him. I mean I tried to reciprocate I really did but I couldn't and he started to know it. He'd ask me what was wrong with me, how could I not care for him when he cared so much? I tried to split up with him but he wouldn't listen. And that's when I came up with my master plan.' Sarcasm and bitterness roiled in her voice and he reached out and took her hand in his, clasped it firmly even when she tried to pull away and that gave her the courage to continue.

'I decided to go to a party and kiss someone else in front of him. In my head that would make the scales fall from his eyes and he'd fall out of love with me and the whole problem would be solved. Ta-da! What actually happened is I did my thing, saw his face and the pain, thought it was working, so I left the party with the man I'd kissed. Then I went home, sure that all would be well. Instead… I found out the next day that Lawrence had overdosed and he would have died if it wasn't for Juno, one of the girls in our group. She'd been worried about him, found him and got him to the hospital in time. I rushed to the hospital and she told me to leave, to get out, I'd done enough damage. I left, and thank God he survived. But he might not have and that would have been my fault, a result of my bad decisions and I regret that with all my heart. But now, now I've heard your story, I truly regret that I've never contacted Lawrence, never said sorry, never explained, because I thought it would make things worse, because he and Juno got together and I hoped they were happy. And I wish that Lawrence had contacted me, demanded an explanation because he deserves one. And so do you.'

He was silent for a while, though his hand

still encircled hers and when he did speak it wasn't the wholehearted agreement she'd hoped for.

'You can't compare what you did to Lawrence to what my mother did to me.'

'I'm not. And I am not trying to excuse what either of us did. But we both made decisions that had profound effects. I could have caused a tragedy, been responsible for a death.'

'You couldn't have known what he would do.'

'But I should have guessed. I knew how much he loved me.'

Max shook his head. 'He was obsessed with you, Stella. That's not love.' He looked at her. 'Is that why you are so adamant you don't want love?'

The question caused her to pause as she looked down at their clasped hands, and then she gave her head a small shake. This was a timely reminder of her stance on love. 'Partly. I don't like what it does to people. Love resulted in my mother being trapped in a marriage of misery, and love sent Lawrence to the abyss. It causes misery not happiness. I don't think anyone's happy ever after should hinge on meeting the "one" and falling in love. In fact it seems…easier to me to find a happy ever after without love. I don't see the point of it. Sure it may work out sometimes but a lot of the time it doesn't. It causes heartbreak and hurt and pain. And… I don't understand it.' That was the truth; love was a mystery to her. Her father professed to love her but that love had been priced, by love he'd meant control. With Lawrence love had become obsession. 'So love is to be avoided.' Again she looked down at their hands, wondered whether she was telling him, or reminding herself. Then realised she'd been distracted from the point.

'But this isn't about love…this is about answers and how you feel about finding your mother.' She waited, hoped he would tell her, share how he felt, but he didn't.

Instead, 'Thank you for telling me about Lawrence. And for what it's worth I get you made some decisions you regret but in the end you didn't intend for what happened to happen—you got in over your head and you tried to get out. But he made the decisions he made and he has to take responsibility too.'

'Thank you. And I promise not to bring it up again. But please don't call off the detectives yet. Sleep on it?'

'OK.'

At least he'd agreed to that, though as she studied his expression, unreadable in the bright light, she wondered if he was humouring her. Knew though that he would keep his word.

He glanced at his watch. 'Right, we need to get going or we'll be late for the party.'

'OK and I'll be right there, by your side. If you feel any sense of panic or anxiety, take my hand.'

He smiled. 'And then what, you'll stamp on my foot with your stilettos.'

'Only in an emergency,' she said as she smiled up at him. 'But I'll wear sandals just in case. *We've* got this. And *we're* going to get this deal.'

He stilled as he looked down at her and then he smiled, a real smile which conveyed warmth and made her feel…ridiculously happy. 'Thank you.' And then he leaned down and, oh, so gently brushed his lips against hers, sending a flutter of sensation though her, a sense of anticipation and hope. 'For everything you've done today.'

He tugged her towards the steps. 'Now let's go party.'

CHAPTER THIRTEEN

'Wow.' STELLA'S VOICE held awe and Max understood why as they stood outside Pria and Rahesh Khatris's Bollywood mansion, a massive sprawling edifice, with Grecian pillars and gleaming whitewashed walls. 'It's… It's hard to believe it's real.' She counted under her breath. 'It's got six stories.'

'Yup, apparently it houses a boxing ring, a gymnasium, a cinema and multiple kitchens and living areas. Oh, and seven bedrooms and a whole room for shoes.'

'Be still my beating heart. Let's go in and check out the inside. And clinch your deal.

'Remember I am by your side with my trusty sandals.' She hitched up the skirt of her grey dress and lifted a foot, to reveal red-and-gold mirrored sandals, the gold thread picking up the glint of the necklace he'd given her.

And as they entered now a tremor of anxiety did threaten, a sudden nightmare entered his brain of hundreds of faceless women walking towards him against a backdrop of party cacophony, all chanting, 'I am your mother', and for a moment his feet dragged. But then Stella's hand slipped into his. 'You've got this,' she whispered and he kept walking.

Knew that next to him Stella was thinking 'double wow' as they both took in the interior. Opulent didn't cover it, though it was opulence with plenty of style. Fluffy rugs were scattered over the highly polished wooden floor, chandeliers hung from the ceilings, there were mirrors and glass, low marble tables, leather sofas, the theme black-and-white, all blending into an aura that screamed no expense spared.

Guests mingled, and tuxedoed waiters worked the crowds seamlessly moving with silver trays laden with champagne and mango juice and carefully crafted canapés. Rahesh and Pria swept up to greet them, and he let himself be caught up in the swing of the party, the atmosphere, the exquisite taste of the canapés. Though that was trumped by watching Stella eat them and her running commentary.

'Amazing… Max you have to try this. They are called *aloo tikki* and they are spiced mashed potato coins. And this…it's called a *puri* shot—and the *puri* are stuffed with black chickpeas in a fresh mint sauce…'

But Stella didn't just eat, she circulated, and he couldn't help but admire the deft touch she had with people, her ability to converse and truly listen. The episode of earlier in the day seemed far behind him until Pria approached him, a smile on her face, 'Max, there you are. Rupali wanted a quick word.'

Rupali, Rupali, Rupali… He was aware of Pria's watchful gaze as the set designer approached and he exhaled in relief as nothing happened—he could see that she was a woman in her midthirties, approaching him with a slightly wary smile on her face.

'Hi, Rupali. I am so glad you are here. I wanted to apologise—I am sorry if I made you uncomfortable—it was unintentional.'

The woman raised her hand. 'It is OK. You don't need to explain.' She smiled, a sweet smile that seemed to encompass understanding. 'And you didn't make me uncomfortable—not once I realised that you weren't really seeing me. And not when I saw Stella stamp your foot. You looked like my grandmother does when she is sleepwalking. So we're good.'

Relief trickled through him.

'And also I have found another Rupali Patel who did study in England. She also works for Rahesh and Pria as well but in the costume department.'

He could picture Stella's eyes widen as she tensed next to him, hear her well-modulated voice say *Really* in his head, with a rising of incredulity as her hand twined firmly round his.

The woman he was now keeping in his head as Rupali One stepped to one side to reveal another smiling woman. Rupali Two and now the nightmare image from earlier resurfaced and he forced himself not to look round for the faceless horde of his imagination.

Next to him Stella held a hand out. 'It's good to meet you, Rupali. When were you in England and where?'

'In Manchester about twenty years ago now.' It couldn't be her and this time Max was able to process that, able now to engage both Rupalis in hopefully intelligent conversation. Thanks in part he knew to Stella's swift intervention, the way she'd got him the information he needed, allowed him to contain the burgeon of panic before it took hold.

Appreciation touched him that she had his back, that she'd persisted earlier, and now she'd done as she promised and been by his side. They made a good partnership. Max frowned, aware that an idea was beginning to seed in his mind; he recognised the foreshadow of a plan, the ping of a possible light bulb above his head. But before he could pursue the trail Rahesh approached, his brown eyes studying Max closely. 'There is going to be an impromptu Bollywood dance, we thought you may both like to watch or better yet join in?'

'I'm in.' Stella's acquiescence was instant and as Max eyed the other man, he realised this was a test of sorts, to assess whether he would fit as a business partner, truly be part of the company that Rahesh had founded and loved and believed in.

'As long as you aren't expecting talent I'm in,' he said. 'But seeing as I am about to make a fool of myself I'd like something in return.' Time to show he really did mean business.

Rahesh nodded. 'That seems fair. What would you like?'

'Agreement that you will discuss the idea of producing some films that also include Western actors and films that don't exclusively star you.'

It was audacious, but it was the one point he hadn't been able to get across or persuade directors to put across to Rahesh and Pria—the directors telling Max that they'd never buy it. 'I know it's not your studio policy but with InScreen we could expand production, it's still your name on every movie and if you want to direct or produce you would still have creative control.'

'All this in return for a dance?'

'It's more than that. This dance is a symbol—I want to mesh our two cultures and businesses. You would still have autonomy and final choice. I wouldn't be able to produce a film you don't like, but I'd like to be able to produce more.'

'I'll talk to Pria—we decide together and I can't say fairer than that.'

'Done.'

Rahesh grinned at him. 'Now let's dance.' The actor headed off towards the dance floor that was set up in one part of the massive space and Max sighed.

Stella glanced at him. 'You don't want to do this do you?'

He shrugged. 'My lessons didn't cover Bollywood so I am about to make a massive fool of myself in front of people I'd quite like to take me seriously. But there are worse things in life. And if he and Pria agree to my terms it will be worth it.'

'We danced really well together last night. Follow my lead and it'll all be good.'

'I like the optimistic approach.'

They headed to the dance floor where Pria and Rahesh stood.

Pria started to speak, 'OK, people, for the benefit of Max and Stella I'm going to say a little bit about the dance and give some tips. You'll know from watching our movies that Bollywood dancing is highly synchronised and the movements are both graceful and energetic.

'The dance also crucially tells a story. So the fluidity of the hand, neck and head movements, the facial expressions are vital. The hand movements are in fact a type of sign language. And of course there are your feet—the moves are pretty complicated so be careful not to trip up! We'll start with a dance called a bhangra, not too hard.'

'So,' Rahesh said, 'Are you ready?'

Stella nodded, her expression serious. 'Can we watch for a few minutes and join in when we're ready.'

'Of course.'

So for the next ten minutes they watched as Pria and Rahesh and about ten of the other guests started a dance, and then Stella said softly, 'I'm going to join them. Watch for a bit longer. Don't worry too much about your feet, focus on arms and keeping to the beat.'

He nodded, watched as she moved into line, saw how easily she fitted in, her body sinuous, energy and grace personified and for a while he was mesmerised as she joined the fluid line of dancers. And as he watched her, saw her give him a quick glance and a sudden wink of encouragement, the idea from earlier put down roots and his brain raced, ran with it, and to the beat of the drums, the repeat pattern of four beats, the idea became a plan, a certainty, a path.

And he knew it was now or never and somehow the enormity of his plan made it almost easy to move in behind Stella, to focus on her, on how she moved so he could emulate it, the sway of her body, the grace with which she extended her arms, the exquisite column of her neck and the ripple of corn-blonde hair. And then following the moves he placed his hand around her waist, felt her falter for the first time before regaining her rhythm and now the tempo increased and Max just did his best to keep up. But all the time as the drums pounded and the movement of the dancers became faster and faster his plan took shape, took life as if given vitality from the exhilaration of the dance.

Then Stella moved gracefully out of line, and he followed suit and they turned and clapped to the beat as the remaining dancers incredibly upped the pace, yet maintained the fluidity of the dance until in synchronised pairs they dropped backwards until it was only Pria and Rahesh to do a grand finale. And at the end the whole room applauded and Max felt the genuine sense of family, understood truly that for Rahesh and Pria their employees mattered.

The couple walked over to them, only barely out of breath.

'Stella you were outstanding…a natural.'

'Thank you, Pria. I loved it… I'll be looking for lessons as soon as I get to London.'

Rahesh shook Max's hand. 'And Max you get points for effort.'

'I'll take that.' With a nod the celebrity couple moved away and Max turned to Stella and they simply looked at each other for a long moment and she was so damned beautiful, her face flushed, her eyes sparkling, her blonde hair ruffled.

'You were incredible,' he said in all sincerity, still blown away by the grace of her movements, the way she'd absorbed the aura, the controlled extravagance of the dance.

'I'd have kept going, but I thought it had probably been enough for the baby.' She grinned. 'Maybe she'll have picked up some moves and will be the next Pria Khatri.'

'Or maybe you will—you definitely impressed everyone here.'

'More important I think you sealed your deal.'

But by now the words were simply a show, said for the sake of saying something. But the real conversation was happening elsewhere, as awareness shimmered and rippled in the air, carried on the notes of the music that still played. And now Max didn't care, had no intention of shutting it down.

'We should leave,' he said, tried to keep his voice businesslike. 'Pria and Rahesh need to decide whether they want to go ahead and they can do that better without me here.'

'Then let's go and say our goodbyes.'

Ten minutes later they exited the mansion and headed to the car where Rahil waited.

'Why don't we go for a walk,' he suggested.

'I'd like that. I'm still pumped full of energy from that dance and...

'How about we ask Nihal to take us to the Gateway of India? It's meant to be beautiful by night.'

'Sure. Sounds good.'

Max's heart beat hard against his ribcage as the car glided smoothly towards its destination.

'Wow again,' Stella said as they walked towards the illuminated Gateway—the loom of the structure glowed golden against the indigo blue of the night sky, and the purple waves of the Arabian Sea. The fifteen-metre dome flanked by four turrets, the whole an architectural fusion of East and West.

'Amazing that it was designed by a Scottish architect, in honour of British royalty.'

'I suppose back then they couldn't have imagined how history would play out.'

'It makes you think though, doesn't it?' he said. 'How much life can change, how things we take for granted, think will last for ever may not. Perhaps it means we should seize the moment.'

She heard an edge to his voice, one she couldn't quite decipher, as they made their way through the still-populated square in front of the Gateway. Late-night street vendors sold their wares to a steady stream of custom and the smell of the sea mixed with the smell of masala chai. Nearby, the magnificence of the Taj hotel also lit up the skyline.

They found a secluded spot by the seawall, near the Gateway itself, close enough that she could see the detail of the inscriptions on the basalt walls, hear the lap of the waves. Leaning against the wall, she turned to him, her eyes open in question.

'Seize the moment how?'

'I think we should get married.'

Say what now? Stella lifted her hand to her jaw to make sure it hadn't dropped to ground level. 'Married?' The word swam around her head, images starting to form. Being with Max, a swirl of confetti in the air, having the baby together. More of the warm fuzzy feelings from today... She blinked fiercely dissipating the pictures before they could take hold, touched her tummy in a reminder of who she needed to think of first and fore-most.

'Yes. Married.' His voice carried convic-tion. 'Co-parenting will be so much easier if we are under the same roof. Otherwise let's say the baby stays with me three nights a week or whatever we decide and the re-mainder with you. It means invariably one or other of us is going to miss milestones, it means our child will effectively have two homes. Getting married means she can have one stable home, it means as well there won't be the added complications of stepfamilies in the mix.'

Stella tried to think; but it was hard be-cause every word he said seemed to make complete sense. The thought of missing her child's first steps, the thought of packing a suitcase every week, for every month, for every year as the child shuttled between homes, conversations over video calls in-stead of in the flesh seemed bleak. But...

'We can't get married just for the sake of the baby, because there is nothing worse for a child than growing up with miserable, war-ring parents.'

'Agreed and I would never wish what you went through on any child. But we won't be miserable, or warring.' His voice deep and reassuring and full of promise. 'Why would we? You said you wanted a marriage where you were partners, where both parties bring something to the table, would be good parents and have liking and respect. We tick all those boxes and we have the extra ingredient as well. Attraction.'

For a fraction of a second unease touched her and then it was gone, as anticipation thrilled through her, as the prospect dizzied her—the magic of that night in Dubai could be hers on repeat. Forever. On tap, whenever she wanted. She reached out, touched his arm, shivered at the feel of solid lithe muscle. Tried to stem the course of desire. 'We can't get married just so we can have sex.'

He smiled, a genuine smile that crinkled his eyes and turned her tummy to mush. 'I thought about that, long and, excuse the pun, hard. And we wouldn't be. I know what it feels like to just want sex and this isn't it. I want the whole package. The respect, the liking, the living under one roof with our child. *And* the sex.'

There was that smile again, and he sounded

so sure, but… 'You've never had a relationship, only interludes.'

'I don't want interludes anymore, not once
we have a baby. I don't want my child to see
me splashed across the papers with an interlude and sure, so far I have mostly managed
discretion but that's not a guarantee for the
future.' He shrugged and her gaze caught on
the breadth and strength of his shoulders, the
ripple of his shirt against his chest and she
gulped. 'The way I see it what's better, an
occasional interlude or us?'

Us. That was the crux of it. They would
be an us. A couple. Perhaps they could have
a couple name. Stellax or Mella or… Or perhaps she should get a grip. 'But it's such a big
commitment. How can you be sure? I know
how resistant you were to marrying Dora
even for two years.'

'That was different. There was no baby.
And Dora wasn't you.' He took both her
hands in his, and now his voice was serious,
his brown eyes dark and intent. 'This is not
a sacrifice on my part, Stella, and I don't
want it to be one on yours. I believe this is
right for the baby. This would give me the
chance to give my child what I craved most
as a child myself. A parent who is present,

is there all the time and a stable happy supportive upbringing. *But* I accept we can still be good parents, bring up a child successfully without marriage. But I think marriage is right for us as well. We would be happy too—I wouldn't suggest this if I thought we couldn't make a go of it.'

Instincts warred within her. Part of her told her this was a no-brainer—every point he'd made, oh, so valid, and he seemed so very sure. Stood there silhouetted in the golden glow from the Gateway, lamplight glinted on the black of his hair shadowing the decisive planes and angles, the strength of his features.

And another part of her was terrified, petrified she'd make the wrong decision, scared, 'What if I can't make a go of it?' she asked now. 'My relationship history is hardly stellar. I was brought up by parents whose marriage was miserable. What if I say yes and then I mess the whole thing up.'

'The past doesn't matter as long as we don't ignore it—as long as we learn from it, acknowledge it. You will bring yourself into our marriage and *you* are a good person, who cares about others. I get how much your relationship with Lawrence has coloured the rest of your life. I think you've lived with the aftermath ever since.' Now he took a step closer to her and she saw the sincerity in the dark pools of his eyes. 'I think after Lawrence you decided that you couldn't be you anymore, that you had to give up your dream to become a lawyer, to have your own life. And so you built a persona, cool, poised, perfect, the Stella Morrison who would become a countess, a Stella who always made the right decisions.' Her eyes widened as his understanding blew her away. 'You don't have to be that persona any more. Whatever you decide you can make that decision as the real you. And whatever you decide I promise I will always try to be the best co-parent I can be.' His grasp tightened round her hands. 'And you don't have to give me an answer now. I get it's a lot to think about and you need to know you're making the right decision.'

And again warmth suffused her at his knowledge that she couldn't, wouldn't rush a decision, not with her track record of disastrous choices.

Words didn't seem adequate at this point and so she did what seemed natural, she closed the gap between them and brushed a kiss against his cheek, inhaled the scent of him, the woodsy cedar soap that mingled with the smell of the sea breeze. But it wasn't enough and they both shifted balance and now she slid her lips from his cheek to his lips, in a gentle imprint, that lingered for a timeless moment as he cupped her cheek in his hand and, oh, so gently deepened the pressure of their lips.

Stella gave a small gasp at the sheer intensity as sensations deepened into a lush sweetness that felt so right, so full of promise. Knowledge pooled and coalesced inside her, a knowledge gleaned from the past hours and days and she knew she'd fallen for him. That she loved this man, and now…now she had the chance to spend her life with him. The realisation sent both joy and fear through her and she knew that now more than ever she did need time, time to make a decision. And so she pulled away, scared that he'd be able to tell somehow and she knew this love had to be kept secret for now.

She studied his face in the starlight, seemed to see him afresh; saw a good man, a man who knew what he wanted and would fight for it. But a man who she knew had his own demons and vulnerabilities. Could he grow to love her? Optimism surged through her. Surely it was possible…

'Penny for them?' he said, and she shook her head.

'No—they aren't worth it. But you've given me a lot to think about.' She summoned a smile, a poised, friendly Stella Morrison–persona smile, aware of the irony but she knew it was vital to keep her revelation private, until she worked out what to do. 'But I promise not to take long. Give me a couple of days.'

CHAPTER FOURTEEN

Two days later

STELLA CLOSED HER eyes in the welcome cool of the evening breeze, tucked a stray tendril of hair behind her ear, looked up at Max who was walking next to her and then down at their entwined hands and happiness clenched inside her.

The past two days had been…full of wonder. They'd talked about anything and everything, nothing deep or meaningful but important things nonetheless. Movies, films, music, antenatal classes, schools, private versus public education, politics, flowers, holiday destinations… They'd eaten, fed each other snacks, and every moment had felt precious, the fact that each one could be a prelude to the rest of her life seemed almost impossible. Max had made some pretext to go back to the jewellery bazaar and Stella couldn't be certain, but she suspected that a ring nestled in his pocket right now. After all where would be a better place to propose than at sunset looking out to sea.

And she'd thought about it, long and hard whilst she'd lain alone in the massive king-sized bed, on silken sheets. Decided that marrying Max was the right choice...because she was happy and she wanted the happiness to continue, because together they could give their child a stable, secure, happy childhood. And as for her love...what did it matter? Yes, she loved him; she'd changed her mind, her attitude to love. Who was to say that Max wouldn't too?

His voice broke into her thoughts.

'Penny for them?'

Now she looked up at him and smiled, saw that he had been guiding their steps towards the seawall, saw too that the sun was just beginning its descent towards the horizon, the sky beginning to move across the spectrum of colour.

'I think they're worth more than that today,' she said softly, knew he would take his cue from those words, saw his hand descend to the pocket of his chinos.

He took a deep breath and his gaze met

hers, direct and unswerving. 'Then here goes. I won't go down on one knee because that would be hypocritical, but I promise I mean every word I am about to say. Stella, will you do me the honour of marrying me? I promise to give you respect and liking and do my very best to make sure our family is a happy one and to give our child, or children a secure, happy, loving childhood.'

He opened the ring box and she looked down at the glint of diamond and gold, opened her mouth to say yes, started the lift of her left hand to accept the ring.

And stopped, as the words of his proposal rang round her head and she realised that she wanted him to go down on one knee. But he couldn't because it would be hypocritical, and Max would never be that. He didn't love her. But that was OK…because one day maybe he would.

Or maybe he wouldn't and then what would happen? Would their marriage go the same way as her parents'? They had started out assuming that they would have a son, that assumption had turned to hope and in the end that hope had withered and died, turned their marriage into a bitter morass of misery.

Would that happen to Stella if Max didn't learn to love her back?

How could it end well; dammit she knew first hand how one-sided love worked out, how it could turn into obsession—would she become like that…as desperate as Lawrence had been?

His voice echoed across the years. *'How can you feel nothing when I love you so much?'*

Max didn't love her. His proposal said it all—he wanted to get married to achieve a happy family unit for the baby. Wanted an agreement founded on a bedrock of liking, respect with a no-love clause baked into that foundation. She'd fallen in love with a man who had no interest in love.

Been foolish enough to put rose-coloured spectacles back on and she had, oh, so nearly walked into a rose-coloured trap that she'd set for herself. Because she couldn't marry Max; couldn't spend a lifetime living a lie, would have to live her life with another persona, couldn't be her real self.

So there would be no romantic acceptance in the sun's setting pink rays; though her heart felt like it might burst, if only she could rip the love out, trample it, accept the proposal in the spirit in which it was given.

The jumble of thoughts whirred through her mind.

'Stella?'

What to say—the truth impossible… Her brain clicked and whirred and she knew she had to resurrect her Stella persona, the poised, cool, aloof model. That Stella would have to take over, spin a refusal he would believe and accept.

'I can't marry you.'

He stepped backwards as though the words had rocked him off balance, his expression one of confusion and the dawn of hurt.

'Why not?'

Max tried to process what the hell was going on. It made no sense and yet there was something in her stance, in her voice that told him she meant it.

'I don't understand,' he said flatly. 'I know you hadn't said yes, but over the past two days every sign pointed that way.'

'I know.' She took a deep breath. 'And I'm sorry. Truly sorry. But…this…' She gestured around them, but he didn't even turn his head, not even the beauty of the sunset could distract him. 'It's not real.'

'Still not getting it. I'm pretty sure I'm real, you're real and the baby is real too.'

'I'm not explaining well. I mean Mumbai—this isn't our reality, where we live, work. How can we decide to spend the rest of our lives together based on a few days here?'

'Fine. I don't think the setting matters, but if you prefer, we'll do this a different way. Go home, spend some more time together, move in together if you want.'

She shook her head, and he saw a hint of panic in her blue eyes, tried to get his head around what was going on. 'It's more than that. I know you aren't like my father. I do. But I don't feel comfortable marrying someone with so much wealth and fame and power.'

He studied her face 'You've known all along who I am and we've discussed this.'

'I know but I still have reservations, questions I haven't answered. If we get married our child will get used to a certain lifestyle, one that you can provide, and if something did happen, if we did decide to split up, where would that leave us?'

'Very well off. I will sign a prenup that

protects you so you are never in the position your mother was in.'

'But that doesn't feel right either. I'd still be living off your money and I don't want that. And there are other things to think about. What would we tell our child about our relationship?'

'The truth.'

'That we got married for them, that's not fair either.'

'But we wouldn't be getting married for the baby's sake—we'd be getting married for all of us, to be a family.'

'It's not enough.' It was as though the words were torn from her, said with a deep pain and truth and now finally the penny dropped as he understood exactly what she was trying to say. He wasn't enough, not for her or for the baby.

Shades of his mother—he hadn't been enough for her. Shades of his foster parents—couldn't they have fought harder; shades of his uncle and aunt—they'd wanted their own child not the 'bad option'. A wave of anger, an echo of how he had felt as a child threatened to tsunami, crashed into the even bigger wave of bleakness because this was different. This was a judgement on him, as he was now. The finished version so to speak and he still wasn't enough.

And that meant losing what he'd achieved with Stella, the warmth, the laughter, the comradeship. All gone. He clenched his fists into his jeans pockets and stared out at the sun as it set on his hopes and dreams. But what could he do? He'd made the deal, that he'd abide by her decision and he would.

So as all the emotions crashed and burned inside him, he pulled himself together, knew that raging and storming would make it impossible for them to move forward as parents. 'I understand.' The words dark and weighed with a bleak truth because he did understand. 'We'll need to work out an agreement. Perhaps it would be best to leave this in our lawyers' hands from here on out. If you truly believe this is best for the baby and best for you then I accept that. This isn't the way I wanted it to pan out, but I hope you find what you're looking for, Stella, find something that is enough.'

She nodded. 'Thank you.' She opened her mouth as though she wanted to say more, settled for, 'For everything.' Her expression drawn and tired, her delicate features etched with sadness.

The walk back to the hotel spent as far apart as possible, such a far cry from just half an hour before when they'd strolled along hand in hand and he'd been so sure that the future held brightness.

A week later

Stella sat opposite her sister in her study in Salvington; relieved that her father had at least thawed sufficiently to allow his eldest daughter over the threshold.

'How is Dad?'

'I saw him earlier, told him you were coming and he asked to see you. He's sleeping now but Mum said she'd come and get you when he's up.'

'Is seeing me a good idea?'

'I think so. The heart attack—it's changed him. He seems more mellow, more resigned to letting things be, accepting the possibility that Salvington may be lost.'

'And are you OK with that? If you and Rob don't have an heir quickly.'

'Yes I am. Like you told me, we can't sacrifice our lives for Salvington. I love Rob, he loves me and we want to spend our lives together. And we deserve the chance to do that without the pressure of having an heir—if it happens great, if not that's OK. We won't let it embitter our lives.' She studied Stella's face. 'Now let's talk about you. Have you decided what you're going to do?'

'I told you.' Her sister had been the first person she'd turned to and she'd told Adriana the whole sorry truth. 'I'm going to get on with my life, focus on being the best parent I can and I am sure Max will do the same.' She tried to inject enthusiasm into her voice. 'I've been in touch with him and we've got our first antenatal class coming up.' The prospect filled her with dread, the idea of being so close to him, of having to pretend, to hide the fact that she missed him with every fibre of her being. 'It will all be fine.'

'It doesn't sound fine. And you don't look fine—you look dreadful.'

'Gee, thanks.'

Adriana shook her head. 'Sorry, but you do, and I'm worried about you.'

'Please don't worry. I don't want to rain on your parade.' And she truly didn't. 'I am so happy for you and Rob.' And she was, even though every word of her sister's story, her happy ending seemed designed to further twist the knife into her own raw sadness. A tale of love and the fairy tale ending. But as she looked at her sister's face, illuminated and radiant with reciprocated love, Stella did feel happy, 'Happy that you finally have the love and recognition and happiness you deserve. And I'm sorry.'

'For what?' Her sister's face creased in genuine confusion.

'Sorry that it took so long, sorry I didn't stand up for you earlier, didn't stand up to Father and call him out for how he treated you. Sorry it's taken me this long to say sorry.'

'Whoa!' Adriana moved over to her sister and gave her a massive hug, held her tight. 'You do not need to be sorry. You have always been the best sister I could wish for.'

Stella shook her head. 'I should have done something.'

'There was nothing you could do. We agreed on the plan—I'd be invisible, you'd keep Dad happy. And listen to me, I think you got the worse end of the deal in some ways. I got to wander around Salvington and do my own thing. You were in the limelight, having to do whatever he said. And, yes, it sucked what Dad did to me, what it did to my self-esteem and confidence but that's on him, not you.'

'You sound like Max.'

Her sister eyed her. 'So you've talked to Max about Dad and about how you feel about things?'

'Yes.' She'd confided things to Max that even her sister didn't know.

'So you trust him?'

'Yes, I do.'

Adriana took her sister's hands. 'Then maybe you should tell him the truth. I know you say you're worried that it will affect how you work together as parents, but from everything you've told me about Max being a dad is too important to him to jeopardise. I don't think he will let it affect how he parents. And neither will you, because you're going to be a great Mum. But if you don't tell him, you're living a lie and you don't deserve that and neither does Max.'

Stella stared at her sister, and knew that her sister was right—that Max did deserve the truth. He'd never got it from his mother, had no idea why she had done what she'd done and Stella herself had told him he deserved answers, deserved the truth. Just as Lawrence had. But Stella had been too scared to tell Lawrence the truth, that she had used him from the start. Too scared to tell her father the truth, that she disagreed with how he treated Adriana. Stella had always walked away. And now… Now she was still scared, and a memory hit of halving her fears and handing them to Max.

She looked up at the tap on the door and her mum entered. 'Your dad would like to see you now, if that's what you want too.'

Max looked down at the unopened letter in his hand; a letter handed over to him by a private detective, along with a report explaining his mother had been located, but didn't want to see him, though she had written him a letter.

Emotions struggled for ascendancy, hurt amongst them. But a hurt that paled beside the pain he'd felt since Stella's rejection, that wound still stung and ached, refused to subside. Constantly prodded by the continuous stream of memories that pretty much anything and everything provoked. A smell of vanilla, a low laugh, a blonde woman, the glint of a gold necklace…any food. Every meal he'd find himself analysing ingredients, thinking of texture, imagining her face as she tasted it.

He blinked, refocused on the letter, part of

him wanted to open it, part of him dreaded the content.

Jeez, Man up, Durante.

Swiftly he ripped open the envelope.

Dear Max,

I am sorry. Sorry I abandoned you and sorry that I cannot see you now.

I was young. Your father tricked me, dazzled me, conned me into believing he was something he wasn't. I couldn't have an abortion, but neither could I keep you as an unwanted reminder of my mistakes.

Soon after your birth I relocated to India—my family brought me here to help me recover.

Many years later I married a good man and we have four children. But I never told him or them about you and I don't want to. He would feel betrayed and it would change everything, all my family relations, and they would see me differently.

So I ask you to please let me be and know I think of you every day and I am proud of your success and take comfort from the fact that your family took you in.

Rupali

Max stared down at the words and then folded the letter up and replaced it in the envelope. Rejected again, gently this time but there had been no doubt in that letter. Rupali wished him well, but she did not want him in her life. An unwanted reminder of her mistakes.

He could hear Stella's voice in his head. 'You're more than that.'

He shook his head. Only he wasn't to Stella—to Stella he wasn't enough.

But there were those words again. 'You're more than that.'

And dammit he was.

He would not let what his mother had done to him, as a baby and now, define him. Not let his uncle and aunt's judgement be the final one. He was more than an unwanted reminder, more than a chip off the old block. And maybe, just maybe he was enough for Stella, if he could find the courage, the strength to be honest. To be real.

And now he knew exactly what he had to do.

Two days later

Stella entered the restaurant where she had arranged to meet Adriana, glanced round in surprise to see how deserted it was, then went to sit at a corner table. Pulled her phone out and looked at the text she was painstakingly composing to Max. Rolled her eyes at her own hesitancy. She had to stop worrying that he would ignore her or refuse to see her. Stop wondering if she should sign it with a kiss.

Instead she pressed Delete, started again.

Hi, Max Could we meet up? Stella

Before she could press Send a waiter approached and she opened her mouth to explain she was waiting for someone. 'Good afternoon. The gentleman at the bar asked me to send this over with his compliments.'

She froze, her heart started to beat a little faster and, oh, so slowly she lifted her gaze to the man sitting at the bar. Dark, dark hair, tamed into a businesslike cut, eyes the colour of expensive chocolate, chiselled features and a jaw that spoke of determination. His body emanated a sense of power and a frisson of pure desire ran through her. She blinked—this wasn't Dubai, wasn't the first time she'd seen him and yet in some ways it felt like she was seeing him anew.

The waiter placed a drink in front of her, 'It's a passion fruit mocktini. And a note.'

She opened the envelope, read the contents. 'I'd like to talk.' That was it and now she looked up and his gaze met hers, unreadable. And then she lifted her glass in a toast and nodded and she saw relief flash across his features.

Then he approached, sat down opposite her and placed his glass on the table. 'Elderflower cocktail,' he said. 'And Adriana says she hopes you don't mind the subterfuge.'

'So you set me up.'

'Yes.'

'You could have just asked.'

He gave the smallest of smiles. 'I thought that lacked pizzazz.'

Her eyes widened and she gave a small breathless laugh. 'In which case I'm guilty of exactly that.' She put her phone on the table, showed him the text. 'I was about to send that.'

A quick scan and he looked at her. 'So who goes first?'

'There's only one way to decide that.' She reached for her purse and pulled out the coin, tossed it in the air as he called tails. 'Tail's it is.'

'Then I'll go first. There is something I want to ask you, something I want to tell you but first, if it's OK I'd like to, I need to tell you some things. About me.'

'Of course it's OK.' Her mind raced, whirred with curiosity, a dawning hope matched by equivalent trepidation.

He paused, frowned as if he was finding it hard to work out what to say or how to say it and she realised he hadn't rehearsed whatever it was. 'I told you that you could be real with me, that you didn't have to hide behind the persona you've created. Well this past week I've come to realise that I've been hiding behind a persona of my own. A success story I wove and spun—the Max Durante who overcame adversity, forgave his mother for leaving him in a cardboard box, was brought up by a loving family and built up a business empire.'

'You are a success story,' she said softly.

'Perhaps, but that's not how it happened. That's the spiel I put together.'

'I don't understand.' But she wanted to, leant forward, her gaze fixed on him, and she saw shadows in his eyes, but determination as well.

'After I was found in the cardboard box

I was put into foster care, with a wonderful couple who I lived with for four years.' Stella held her breath, knew that this was something he had kept to himself, there had been no mention of this in any of his interviews. 'I can still remember them, remember a feeling of safety and warmth. They had just started proceedings to adopt me and then my uncle and aunt turned up. My uncle was my father's older brother. Carlos and his wife Annalise.'

'But surely by then you were bonded to your foster family.'

'I was but Carlos was my real family and blood trumped all. Also they were younger than my foster carers, they didn't have any kids of their own and they said they desperately wanted to adopt me. There was also my grandmother in the picture and she was very keen on the idea.'

'So they were allowed to adopt you?'

'Yes. Though it took time. I was removed from my foster carers and put with other carers whilst proceedings went ahead.' His dark eyes shadowed and she knew he was no longer seeing the restaurant in front of him, or the people on the busy London street outside. Instead he was reliving a tragic memory, and as he spoke she could see the small dark-haired boy he must have been, clinging to the people he'd known as parents, the people he loved. Being wrested away by unkind hands, dragged kicking and screaming away. To land in a strange, unfamiliar house with strange, unfamiliar people however kind and months later taken again to another place and told this was home.

'It didn't feel like home. I was five by then, and confused and sad and so very angry. With everyone. My old foster carers for "abandoning me", and my uncle and aunt for taking me.'

Stella blinked back tears, gently placed her hand on his arm, wished with all her heart she could go back in time and try to somehow explain things to the poor little boy. 'Were you allowed to see your foster carers?'

'No. I was told a clean break was better.'

'And your uncle and aunt? Carlos and Annalise?' she asked, could hear the desperate sound of hope in her voice. 'What were they like?'

'On the plus side they did provide me with food and clothing and a roof over my head. But adopting me was a mistake. They didn't really want to do it, they told me later my grandmother forced them to do it, threatened to disinherit them if they didn't. My father was the black sheep of the family and Carlos and Annalise hated him, but my grandmother had adored him, right up to the point he died in a prison brawl when I was four. That was when they found out about me. Carlos and Annalise couldn't have children of their own and I was a poor substitute, especially as my grandmother died very soon after the adoption went through. To them I was a chip off the old block, a carbon copy of my father. My father the career criminal. A liar, a womaniser, a gambler, a cheat…a drug user who ended up in prison on numerous occasions; he also had immense charm, charisma and good looks. Apparently I am the spitting image of him. And they believed that I was intrinsically bad and destined to follow in his footsteps.'

'Oh.' This was so warped, so horrible and Stella's hand clenched into fist. 'But that is so wrong.'

'In their defence my behaviour was appalling—I was so confused and angry that I lashed out, tried to run away, broke things… and it all fed into their beliefs. Plus they never wanted me anyway.'

'But how can you bring a child up to believe they are bad?' She couldn't wrap her head around it. 'You weren't your father, you were you and of course you were angry, you were tiny, a child, and… *I* am so…angry.'

'It wasn't all their fault.'

'How can you say that?'

'They hated my father. I mean really loathed him. And I think they had cause to. From what they told me there was no depth he didn't sink to and yet my grandmother always forgave him even though it was Carlos who did well, who studied hard, who did the right thing. But he couldn't provide her with a grandchild like my father did. They looked at me and they saw him. Just like my mum.' And again she sensed he was back in the past, looking back at a childhood strewn with cruelty. 'My aunt told me that my mum must have taken one look at me and she must have seen it in my eyes. That I was destined to be like my father.'

This got worse and worse. 'That isn't true.' But the young Max must have believed it was, maybe on some level he still did. 'If you look like him that is genetics, what is inside you…it's you. And you have made your own destiny and it is clearly nothing like your father's. Surely they must have seen that.'

'Nope.' He shook his head. 'I don't think anything could shake their convictions about me. When I was sixteen they asked me to leave, said their duty was done. Years later when I was beginning to be successful I contacted them, because I still hoped that maybe they would change their minds. But they wouldn't even see me. Said something along the lines of success doesn't make you a good person.'

'That must have hurt.'

'Yes, it did, though I didn't want to admit it even to myself—I told myself I didn't care, told myself I was bigger than all that, that I was successful, wealthy, ambitious. So it didn't matter what they thought. And so I built my persona, to hide the fact that inside I've always felt diminished. My mother had rejected me without even knowing me, and my aunt and uncle rejected me no matter what I did to try and win their love, or even their liking and that made me feel small, inadequate and I hid that behind the aura of success. And I decided that I wouldn't let anyone reject me again. Then I had a double whammy. You rejected my offer and then the detectives found my mother and she wrote me a letter. She doesn't want to be contacted, she's married with other kids, and she wants to keep her status quo as it is.'

'Max. I…'

'No. It's OK. Because it made me think. Rupali Patel is technically my mother, but she doesn't know me, she isn't rejecting me, or judging me because she doesn't know me. My aunt and uncle never bothered getting to know me—all they could see was the image they created, a mini version of my father. But you…that was different. You rejected me.

'And you were right. What I offered you *wasn't* enough, a marriage of convenience, a sham marriage, a persona of a marriage, built on a contract. I offered you the Max Durante persona because I was too scared that the real me wouldn't be enough, too scared to admit how I really feel.'

'How do you really feel?' Her heart pounded and hope burgeoned inside her.

'I love you.' The words tumbled out of him. 'I don't expect you to reciprocate, but I love you. I love you, the real Stella, the woman who cares for other people and wants to make a difference, the woman who tastes every item of food as though it is the most important thing in the world. I love your smile, your laugh, the way tears sparkle in your eyes. I love the way you give everything your all, the way you truly listen to people, the way you've made me re-evaluate and think about who I am. And I want to marry you, not for the baby's sake, but because I want to spend the rest of my life with *you*. I understand if that's not what you want, but I want you to know, know that's how I feel.'

Stella opened her mouth tried to find the right words amongst the tumult of happiness that jumbled inside her. 'But that's why I said I couldn't marry you.' Seeing his look of confusion she stopped, knew she'd better get the most important fact across. 'I love you. I am totally completely head over heels in love with you.'

'You are?'

But even as she saw happiness begin to light up his brown eyes she sensed a hesitancy. 'You promise this isn't because you feel sorry for me, don't want to reject me out of some misguided compassion.'

'I promise. I wouldn't insult your honesty with that sort of "compassion". I love you. That's what I wanted to talk to you about, what I wanted to tell you. I refused your proposal because I love you and I couldn't go ahead with a marriage where I loved you but you didn't love me.

'I should have told you the truth in Mumbai but I was too scared, scared that it would mess up our co-parenting. And so for the past days I have tried to do the right thing. I started work and I've talked about paint and colour themes with a smile on my face, I've helped Adriana with wedding plans with a smile on my face. I saw my Dad.' She thought back to the conversation as she told it to Max. Her father looking so frail lying propped up on pillows. His voice soft as he spoke.

'I wanted to say I'm sorry for our last meeting. Nearly dying has changed some of my perspectives on life and I want to live whatever I have left differently. I'm just not sure how yet.' Even those sentences had tired him and Stella had stepped forward and kissed her father on her cheek.

'I know you'll work it out. But now focus on getting better.'

He'd covered her hand and squeezed it before falling back to sleep.

Now she looked at Max. 'And his words made me think, and I realised I wanted that for me too. To live the rest of my life differently. As the real me. And the real me loves the real you. And I realised that *you* are committed to our baby, that you would make being a Dad work no matter what, because you love our baby and you will be the best Dad in the world. So I could tell you the truth. That I love you… The real you, because I could see the real you just like you could see the real me. I love the man who cared enough about me to take half my terror and fear away on the aeroplane when he was in shock himself, the man who makes me laugh, the man who cares so much about his child. The man who showed me vulnerability, who confided in me to help me. And, yes, the man who has made so much of his life, who has drive and power and ambition, who is a success. The man who danced a Bollywood dance, the man who told me I could be a lawyer, could follow my dream. The man I want to spend the rest of my life with, wake up with every morning. I love you and if the coin had fallen differently I would have told you first, because you are enough, you've always been enough for me. I love you with all my heart.'

And now he plunged his hand into his

pocket and in an instant he was in front of her, down on one knee.

'Stella Morrison, will you marry me? I promise to love you for the rest of our lives, to cherish you and talk to you and share the ups and downs. I want to raise our family together and I swear I will always be there for you, the real me with all my flaws and vulnerabilities and all my strength.'

'Yes. I will marry you and I will be there for you, stand by your side. Always. We will be a happy family full of love for each other, and I will always be there to share the good times and the harder times, the real me. I will never walk away from us.'

And then he slipped the ring onto her finger and she knew that this was the happiest moment of her life, knew that this choice was the best one she could ever make.

EPILOGUE

STELLA TOOK MAX'S hand as they entered Salvington Manor, ducking under the festoon of pink balloons that adorned the top of the front door.

'Look at that Bea,' Stella said. 'Balloons.'

The baby safely ensconced in the forward-facing baby carrier strapped securely around Max's chest gave a gurgle of laughter and Stella leaned over to drop a kiss on her daughter's downy-haired head. 'Balloons,' she said again, 'to celebrate your cousin Martha's christening.'

'Welcome.' Rob stepped forward, holding Martha in his arms, his face so full of pride and happiness that Stella's heart turned as she kissed her brother-in-law's cheek and watched as the two men exchanged a complicated handshake. 'Your parents and Adriana are in the living room along with some of the other guests.'

Before they could follow him, there was a knock at the door and Stella stepped forward to open it, gave a beaming smile as she saw the identity of the guests. 'Maxine, Chris. I'm so glad you're here.'

'Me too,' Max stepped forward and hugged the elderly couple, the foster carers who had looked after him for the first years of his life, released them as Rob reappeared and led them into the living room.

Stella held back for a moment and turned to Max. 'I'm so glad you contacted them.'

'So am I.' He smiled down at her. 'One of your excellent ideas.'

'But you did it.' And she knew it hadn't been easy, knew he'd feared rejection, believed that maybe Chris and Maxine hadn't really wanted to adopt him all those years ago. But it turned out they had wanted to, had fought as hard as they could until eventually they had backed down only because social services had convinced them his uncle and aunt were a better option for Max.

And over the years they'd assumed that decision to be correct, but *'It didn't stop us from missing you, loving you, thinking about you,'* Christine had said, tears spilling from her eyes at their first meeting. And since then they had become honorary grandparents.

'Which shows what a good team we are,' Max said now as he took her hand in his to enter the living room where more balloons bobbed from the ceiling, all pink. Every decoration a signal that a daughter was a welcome addition to the family.

Stella's gaze flickered to her father, who was listening to something his wife was saying; he nodded and smiled and then headed over to where Adriana had just taken Martha from Rob.

In truth Stella was unsure as to how her father truly felt about the fact that both his daughters had produced daughters, but all credit to him—Lord Salvington did seem to be trying hard to be a better person, a better father and a good grandfather.

Her father beckoned to her and she walked across, scooping Bea from Max as she did so, love swelling inside her along with confusion. How could Rupali have abandoned Max, how could her own father have taken a dislike to Adriana?

Lord Salvington nodded as Stella approached.

'I want to say something to you both, your husbands too.'

In an almost synchronised movement Rob took Adriana's hand as Max took Stella's and Stella was almost tempted to smile as she saw the protective aura that surrounded both men.

'I've made many mistakes in my life,' her father said. 'But I'd like to not make any more. I want both you girls to know that I will do my best to be a good grandfather to both my granddaughters. And your mother and I have decided we are going on a cruise as soon as the doctors give me the go-ahead, and if I can persuade her to give me another chance I will, but if I can't, I won't stand in her way.'

Stella saw he looked pale, but before she could move Adriana was there, an arm around him and Stella smiled at her sister, admired anew her kindness and capacity to forgive and care. But everyone deserved a second chance and when there was so much love in this room for these two beautiful, gorgeous, precious babies and so much happiness she hoped with all her heart that in their later years her parents could maybe rediscover love.

As for herself and Max and Adriana and Rob, Stella knew they were embarking on the rest of their lives, together with a guaranteed happy ever after. That was the deal and they would all make sure they kept it.

* * * * *

If you enjoyed this story,
check out these other great reads from
Nina Milne

Falling for His Stand-In Fiancée
Second Chance in Sri Lanka
The Secret Casseveti Baby
Whisked Away by the Italian Tycoon

All available now!